This special signed edition
is limited to 1500 numbered copies
and 26 lettered copies.

This is copy _910_.

WRONG THINGS

WRONG THINGS

Poppy Z. Brite
and Caitlín R. Kiernan

Subterranean Press 2001

Wrong Things

FIRST EDITION
November 2001

ISBN
1-931081-25-5

Subterranean Press
P.O. Box 190106
Burton, MI 48519

email:
subpress@earthlink.net

websites:
www.subterraneanpress.com
www.poppyzbrite.com
www.caitlin-r-kiernan.com

TABLE OF CONTENTS

For Peter and Susan Straub

THE CRYSTAL EMPIRE

by Poppy Z. Brite

"Something huge is going to happen today," Matthew told me.

I couldn't imagine so. We weren't even dressed yet. Late in the morning, in an upstairs room of the big decrepit house we shared with four other people, we lay on a mattress that had once been soaked in a flood and still bore creeping funguslike water stains. Ever since the first time I slept on that mattress, I'd wondered whether mildew was growing inside it; I often thought I detected the musty odor drifting past my nostrils in the dark. It never seemed to bother Matthew.

I spread myself as wide as possible across the mattress, a starfish missing a limb, and let the sun filtering through our dirty window melt over me. It drenched my legs, my hips, my belly. When it began to run between my nipples, I said, "What will happen?"

Matthew propped himself on one elbow and ran his fingers through my hair. "You need a shower," he told me.

"What will happen today?" I asked again.

His fingers gripped the sides of my chin, tightened slightly, threatened pain before letting go. "I haven't found out, Zee. Not yet." Draping our quilt like a long patchwork cape around his shoulders, he rose in a fluid motion and went to the window. He glanced at the street below, then turned his attention to the collection of glass suncatchers hanging from the frame. When we moved into the house, the crystals had already been there, forgotten by someone who'd left in a hurry, suspended from colored threads or gold filigree chains in our bedroom window where they shattered sunlight and flung it in tiny sharp arrows to the corners of the room.

"Are you going to shower?" Matthew asked, his eyes fixed on a crystal heart.

"Yes...no. We're out of shampoo."

"Well, I don't like the way your hair smells. Use dish soap or something."

"I don't have any money. I filled up the car — we'll need gas to get to the show tonight."

"Is Susan still working at that restaurant? Did she get paid?"

"I don't know."

"Get five dollars from Susan. Tell her I said to give you five dollars." Matthew turned abruptly from the window and stared at me until I nodded. Then he came back to the mattress and knelt above me, a knee on either side of my chest. He grabbed a handful of my hair and pulled my head back so that I must look at him. "Remember me, Zee. Remember my face."

"You're not going anywhere...are you?" Suddenly I was afraid.

"Just look at me."

I studied him, trying to see something I hadn't noticed a thousand times before. His jaw was strong, his nose sharp and arrogant, his dark blue eyes very serious. He'd recently cropped his curly brown hair, curbing some of its wildness. His lips looked soft, but had a faint cruel quirk, a hint of the teeth behind them. More than once he had bitten my lip hard enough to draw blood. He stared at me with that clear-eyed calm expression that seldom changed; it hadn't changed last night as he fucked me and it didn't change now, with his hand twined painfully in my hair.

"You'll always remember my face?" he said.

"I couldn't forget it."

"Remember the way I look *now*. Something huge is going to happen—something huger than you can conceive of, Zee. It will change me. You know my face better than anyone else, so I trust you to remember the way I look now. You may not notice the changes at first—they'll come subtly, they'll be stealthy. Then one day you'll look at me and see that I'm a whole new person. Can you remember me the way I am now?"

"Yes."

"Thank you." He bent and kissed me so softly that I hardly knew his lips were on mine until the

11

moist warmth of his tongue flicked across my lips. I wanted to pull him down to me, but I did nothing. Matthew made those decisions.

He crawled to the edge of the mattress and began picking through an enormous heap of clothes. A pair of underwear sailed toward me. "Zee. Are those clean?"

I raised them to my face and inhaled deeply. Nothing but the bleached smell of cotton and an antiseptic detergent ghost. I tossed them back to Matthew. "Yeah, they're clean."

He stepped into the underwear, pulled the quilt more tightly around his broad shoulders, and left the bedroom. I heard someone coming down the hall. "Zee needs five dollars," Matthew said. "Would you go in and give it to her, please?"

Susan came in, pushed some of the clothes out of the way, and sat cross-legged on the bare wooden floor next to the mattress. She was a furtive snaky-haired girl who could have been seventeen or thirty. She had a fresh piercing in her left eyebrow, the flesh red and crusted around the stainless steel ring. From one of her hands dangled an ancient, filthy five-dollar bill. I reached for it, but she jerked it away. "First you have to tell me a secret."

"What kind of secret?"

"Something about Matthew."

"What?"

Susan squirmed, fidgeted. I could not tell if she was uncomfortable, since this was her normal demeanor. "I heard. I heard he can come as many times as he wants to, every night."

I just looked at her, trying to match Matthew's cold gaze. "Give me the money, Susan."

She gnawed her lower lip, which was already chapped and ragged. "You don't give the orders around here."

"No — Matthew does, and if he said for you to give me that money, then you better give it to me. I'll tell him if you don't, and I'll tell him what you asked about him, too."

"No need for that," Matthew said.

Susan jerked around. Matthew was lounging against the doorjamb. He had traded the colorful quilt for a snowy terrycloth bathrobe that was belted loosely around his waist, showing off his rangy, lightly muscled body. I remembered that the bathrobe had come from the thrift shop stained dingy yellow, but Matthew had gotten one of the girls to soak it in bleach over and over again, until it was spotless and pure. His arms were folded across his chest, his hands tucked into the baggy sleeves like a mandarin's.

He nodded at Susan. "Do what I told you. Give Zee the money."

"Sorry, Matthew," Susan said. Her hand shook and the bill drifted lazily to the floor.

"Never mind. Pick up the money and give it to her."

Susan wiped the bill on her grimy jeans before she put it in my hand.

"Thank you, Susan. The problem is that Zee doesn't smell so good. She needs your five dollars to buy shampoo."

"Why can't she use her own damn money?" I knew Susan wanted to buy some meth, and she'd probably saved up just enough; this would wreck her plans for the weekend.

13

"She spent it all on gas so we could drive to the show tonight. You wouldn't want to miss the show, would you, Susan?"

Susan shook her head sullenly.

Matthew's eyes met mine, and a tiny smirk played around his mouth. He looked back at Susan. "Do you even know who we're going to see?"

"The Izzle—" She gnawed her lip again. "The Isle of Man. That's the name of the band."

"I doubt you've heard them, Susan."

"No," she admitted.

"They may be too heady for you. They don't write songs about shooting up and fucking. Teenage gyrations, if you will, fail to captivate them. They're storytellers, magic-weavers. Their singer's voice is like the crystals in the window. I don't know if he realizes it yet, but he has something to tell me."

Matthew went back to the window, stepping gracefully over the pile of clothes, and stood stroking the gold wire of a suncatcher. Susan crawled over to our boombox in the corner of the bedroom and started shuffling through Matthew's CDs. Most of them were classical music, Bach and Vivaldi, which bored her; Susan responded mainly to music with a beat that matched the drug in her bloodstream. Finally she pulled out the Isle of Man's CD, recorded on a tiny independent label here in the city. The four musicians were pictured on the front, blurry; all that could be seen of the singer, Anthony LaGuerre, was a wide grin and a pair of dark eyes half-hidden beneath a mop of blonde hair.

"Is this their only album?" Susan asked.

Matthew nodded. "It doesn't matter if they ever make another. This one says everything."

"Can we listen to it?"

"No. I need to talk to Zee. You'll hear them tonight."

Susan eased herself awkwardly out of her cross-legged position and headed for the door. Without turning from the window, Matthew said quietly, "Susan."

I saw her shoulders twitch. "What—"

"Put the CD back where it was."

She had left it on the floor. With a wild terrified glance at Matthew's back, she shoved it into the CD rack and darted out of the room. Matthew's face was reflected faintly in the dirty glass of the window. He was not smiling, but he looked content.

"Did you hear what Susan said to me?" I asked. "The secret she wanted to know about you?"

"Yes."

"How would anybody know that?"

Matthew turned to me, that little smile still playing around his lips. "The walls in this old house are like ricepaper. She must have heard." He stepped toward me, put one slim bare foot against my chest, and pushed me down onto the mattress. I gave no more thought to what Susan or the walls might hear.

⚭

From the moment Anthony LaGuerre opened his mouth, I could feel Matthew wanting him.

Matthew's eyes darkened, and his hands clutched each other in his lap, and he wanted LaGuerre more than he had ever wanted me or anyone else. I was sure of it. I didn't know what kind of wanting it was; whether it was wanting to make love or to talk soul-

15

deep with LaGuerre or to shut him up in a little jeweled box and let his voice escape when Matthew turned the key, like a golden clockwork nightingale, I couldn't tell.

The club was in a dark cellar full of the ghosts of spilled beer and people's breath. The stage was striped with silver duct tape and walled off with a row of amps. All of us from the house had found spots right up front. Matthew's hand rested lightly on my back. The other four—Susan, two girls both called Jennifer, and an old cokehead guy whose name I always forgot—were clustered behind us. Matthew ignored us all, his calm eyes fixed on the stage, waiting.

When the band came onstage, all four at once, sparse applause spattered the air. Anthony LaGuerre's blonde hair was tousled and silky-looking, and he wore a red shirt whose sleeves were too long, so that he had to keep pushing them back to grip the microphone. He stared out at the club for a moment, and his dark eyes met mine, but nothing registered: he didn't know me. Then he opened his mouth wide, wide enough so that I could see his pink tongue and the two rows of small white teeth, and he breathed in the humid air of the club and sent it out again, and flying away on his exhalation was a sound so desperate, so lovely that every hair on my body prickled in sympathy. LaGuerre must *have* to sing, I thought, because if he kept that waterfall jumble of notes in him for more than a few days, the pressure would surely burst him wide open. I looked sideways at Matthew. He was leaning forward over the edge of the stage, his expression tense, his lips slightly parted, the tip of his tongue caught between his teeth.

LaGuerre held his single clear note for perhaps eight beats. Then his voice soared upward and the rest of the band joined him with their own sounds. They were competent, but any backing band short of the Beatles would have seemed a backdrop for LaGuerre's gorgeous voice. Matthew's lips were moving now, whispering the lyrics along with LaGuerre:

"Don't come to my house, I won't be there
I'm at the temple, the screaming psyche's lair
A night will come when the moon is black
When demons flee not looking back
A night will come when the spheres must cry
The stars will lie
And the innocent die
The underworld is burning and rising..."

It was trite art-rock stuff as far as I could figure, the kind of music that would have sounded cheesy even in the seventies. But Matthew was utterly captivated. Perhaps it was just that sweetly husky, amazing voice. Anthony LaGuerre sang like a man who had lived a thousand years without being sullied by the world. He sounded like milk and wild clover honey, like blue flowers with hearts of purest gold. It didn't matter what words he sang; his voice contained the wisdom of age and the wonder of childhood. Its magic was the magic of the ancient, heady spices in the hands of the three Kings; its despair was the despair of a charred planet whirling aimlessly in the blankness of space; its beauty was without measure.

Matthew began to shiver with desire, and LaGuerre's song mingled with Matthew's wanting to form a hot white syrup that seemed to cover me until I could hardly breathe through the sticky haze. Time slipped by without anyone caring. My nerves twitched and burned. Seconds before I thought they must tear their way out of my skin and fall twitching on the dirty floor of the club, LaGuerre stopped singing. He waited for our applause to die down, and in a low, shy, remarkably unremarkable speaking voice he offered us his thanks.

"We're the Isle of Man, and we hope you've enjoyed the show so far. I'm Anthony LaGuerre — " He grinned as another wave of applause drowned him out. "This is Mike Gantt on guitar — " The tall red-bearded man strummed softly and bowed to the audience. "Bill Roy on the drums — " The drummer twirled a stick. "And Nina Fox on bass." The thin redhead was the only member of the band who looked as young as LaGuerre. As she was introduced she flashed a smile at the crowd, but her hands remained on the neck of her bass.

LaGuerre tried to adjust his mike stand and nearly knocked it over, earning a snort of laughter from the drummer. "This is a song we just finished," he said. "It's about the playwright Christopher Marlowe, who was murdered in 1593. We hope it'll be on our next record."

I couldn't help it; I laughed. How pretentious did you have to be to write a rock song about *Christopher Marlowe*? Matthew's eyes flicked sideways for a bare instant. Then he was looking back at the stage, ignoring me, not even giving off anger; still, I knew I would pay for the lapse later.

18

"A sordid room—a look—a word—a leaden gleam," LaGuerre was singing. "A long streak of blood blazing in the firmament—an inconvenient spirit banished. *Or so the dark gods hope!*" His mouth was wide open; he shrieked the last six words. The instruments crested together in one final sparkling explosion of music. LaGuerre's eyes seemed to glow in the stagelight. His nervousness was gone now, but I thought he must be trembling with joy. His eyes met mine again, and I saw something like love in them—at that moment, I thought, Anthony LaGuerre loved me and everyone and everything in the universe. His elation and my own cynicism suddenly made me feel jaded, old.

The show was over. The band left the stage as humbly as they had come, and I was left with Matthew beside me, clutching my arm, his fingers digging in so hard that I knew I would find five small bruises there later. Before the applause had begun to die, Matthew was pushing away from the stage, weaving through the crowd toward the hallway that led backstage. He didn't let go of my arm, so I had no choice but to follow.

An unshaded bulb high above us lit only the black-painted ceiling. I smelled beer more ripe and rotten than any beer had ever been meant to be. Matthew pulled me along the corridor toward a strip of light wavering under a door at the end. Just as we reached the door, it opened and a girl came out—one of the bartenders. Her face was a pale uncertain blotch in the half-darkness, every feature outlined in dark makeup; she looked like a child wearing the mask of a forty-year-old woman.. "Excuse me—" she said.

"Excuse *me*," Matthew interrupted.

She looked up at him, and paused — he was pinning her with that calm, cold stare, the one I knew so well. "I don't think you're supposed to be back here. The band was very clear about not seeing anyone after the show."

"I don't want to bother them, and I don't particularly need to see them." An icy edge had slipped into Matthew's voice. "I don't have time tonight. I only wanted to get their contact information. My father is an agent with William Morris — he handles the Desert Peaches and Katy Scream. There's a chance he might be interested in repping the Isle of Man, if they're looking for management."

He had caught the girl's attention. Pinned above her left breast was a badge bearing the legend "Mr. Hammer and Mr. Saw," the title of Katy Scream's latest album. "Well. Look. I can't let you see the band. They have some kind of thing about talking to people after shows — I was just taking them beer myself. But I'll see if they have a card or something."

She slipped back through the door. A minute later she returned with a sheet of purple paper. "This is their press release. The singer's managing them right now — that's his address and number on there. OK?"

"Yes. Thank you. That's very helpful." Matthew folded the sheet and slid it into his pocket. As I followed him back into the club, I couldn't help asking, "Does your father really have anything to do with music?"

"My father is dead."

Over the crowd I saw Susan and one of the Jennifers waving to us. Matthew put a long arm around my shoulders and steered me toward the exit.

The other Jennifer and the cokehead were sprawled across the back seat of the car making a half-hearted attempt at sex. When Matthew leaned in and spoke quietly to them, they pulled their clothes together, hopped out the opposite door, and crammed into the front with the other two girls. Matthew and I always rode alone in the back seat.

As Susan drove out of the parking lot, Matthew told her, "Zee needs to stop at a drugstore on the way home. Her hair smells like lemons now, and I don't like that any better than I liked dirt."

I shivered.

"Are you cold, Zee?" He put his hand on my back. "Here, take my jacket." I slid forward and he helped me into it, enveloping me in black silk that hung nearly to my knees. It was drenched with the smell of his skin, spicy and faintly sharp. His fingernails scratched against the rough cloth draped over my thighs. His lips brushed my ear. A wave of pleasure welled up from my stomach, soaking me, warming me like liquor. Matthew's mouth covered mine, hot and sweet. When our lips unlocked my tongue was laced with numbness, as if I had gulped a cup of scalding tea.

Yellow light flooded the car. The front wheels hit a concrete divider and we came to an abrupt halt. The drugstore. "Come in with me," I said, but Matthew shook his head, as if he hadn't been kissing me a moment ago.

"Shampoo," he said. "Oh, and Zee? Get a razor. Not one of those cheap disposable things. A straight razor."

The store was incredibly bright after the darkness of clubland. The glare of the fluorescent lights hurt my eyes so badly that I couldn't read the signs above the aisles. I nearly walked into a rack of gaudy plastic sunglasses. Shades would be good right now, I decided; I would get some shades. I selected a mirrored pair and balanced them on my nose.

"Can I help you with something?"

The manager had come up behind me without my noticing. He must have been watching me since I came in, I thought as I saw the suspicion in his piggy bloodshot eyes. "Can I *help* you?" he repeated in that tone store workers sometimes use, not really an offer of help as much as a warning that they've got their eye on you.

"Do you carry straight razors?" I asked.

"You mean the old-fashioned kind? No, I don't know where you could buy one of those any more. They're dangerous." He paused a shade too long. "If you want razors for shaving, they're on aisle three."

It didn't really matter. I knew I didn't have enough money for such a thing, and the manager would be watching me now. Since Matthew had told me to get a razor, I selected the cheapest pack of disposable ones, then found the brand of shampoo whose scent Matthew liked. After paying the girl at the register, I had enough change left over for a peppermint patty, and was standing near the exit unwrapping it when I saw the pig-eyed manager coming for me again. "Just a minute. I don't think you paid for those sunglasses."

I'd forgotten I was wearing the mirror shades, and I knew I didn't have enough money left to pay for them. The manager would call the police, and Matthew would tell Susan to drive away when he saw them pull up. He'd think I had betrayed him; that would be the worst part.

I lunged toward the exit, but the manager grabbed the back of Matthew's jacket. I wriggled out of it entirely and threw myself at the exit door. My head hit the door so hard that I heard a hollow explosion in my skull. The sunglasses clattered away. I pushed myself up on all fours and tried to scramble away from the manager. Behind me, I heard the entrance door gliding open—the police already? I collapsed on my side, plastering my hands over my eyes. The floor was gritty but mercifully cool against my cheek. From very far away I heard Matthew say, "Zee?", then "What did you do to her?"

"What did *I* do to *her*?" The clerk sounded angry, but also a little scared now. "Your girlfriend here tried to shoplift, and when I stopped her, she freaked out and cracked the glass with her goddamn *head*!"

"I see. And when did you rip her jacket off?"

"She ripped it off herself, trying to get away from me."

"Is that true, Zee?" Matthew made me look up at him, telling me what to say with his eyes.

I let myself start to cry. It was a horrible feeling, worse than vomiting, but I knew Matthew needed me to do it as part of his plan. "No," I said with a little hitch in my breath. "He just grabbed me."

Matthew let me go, turned to the manager, and grabbed him by the ear. He had only used this move on me a couple of times, but I knew how painful it was. "Do you want to tell the police about it?" he asked the man.

"It's bullshit—let me *go*, you cocksucker—"

"I'll call them myself."

23

"No—forget it—just get her out of here." I saw tears start in the manager's eyes, and Matthew gave his ear a final twist, then left him go. He retreated down the nearest aisle. "Crazy fucking bitch," he said when he was a safe distance away.

Matthew ignored the man. He stood staring down at me, his expression oblique. I could not hold his eyes. I looked at the floor and saw my forgotten peppermint patty smeared across the tiles beneath his shoe. When I looked back up, I thought he might hit me. Instead he wrapped his arms around me and pulled me close. I buried my face in his shirt, in his familiar clean smell. "I was so scared," I said. "I thought you'd let the police take me."

"You thought I wouldn't come for you?" Matthew stroked my back. "I'd never let them take you, Zee. As long as I want you, there's no way anyone can keep me away from you. Don't you know that?"

"The sunglasses—"

"Fuck the sunglasses." They lay on the floor nearby. Matthew checked to make sure the manager was still watching us from a distance; then he stepped on the sunglasses and ground the mirrored plastic into shards with his heel. The manager looked away.

When he had led me to the car and we were headed home, Matthew took the plastic drugstore bag out of my hands. "Did you get the straight razor?"

"They didn't have a straight razor. I got a package of the disposable ones."

Matthew's eyes trapped mine. His face was absolutely still. I had seen him look at Susan and the others this way, but the look was seldom trained on me. "Did I tell you to buy disposable razors?"

"No, but—"

"Did I tell you to waste money on a bunch of cheap plastic sticks that are dull after you use them once? I thought you knew by now to do what I tell you." His hand slid under the voluminous jacket and found my breast. His fingers closed on the nipple, pinched, twisted. The sensation shifted from a sharp pain to a searching, twisting throb. An instant before I thought I would scream, he let go. "I really thought you knew better than that by now. If you wanted these worthless things so much, you can come back here and look for them tomorrow." He cranked the window down a few inches and fed the package to the passing windstream. I rested my chin on the back of the seat, smelling dimly the sour-milk odor of Susan's old car, and watched the razors dwindle in the rear window. I thought of other cars running over them and cracking them. The pink package shimmered faintly against the black ribbon of road. When I could no longer see the razors, I laid my head on Matthew's shoulder and didn't open my eyes again until we were home.

☙❧

Time had doubled back when I woke the next day, or so it seemed: the first sensation that reached me, even before I opened my eyes, was the sound of Anthony LaGuerre's voice raised in bittersweet song.

"Your words slice me, oh
They may as well
Since I cannot tell
And I cannot go
You need not think your presence matters

For you've built a private grotto in my brain
I know you'll be here with me ever
And it's only in the next world I can find sur-
cease from pain — "

A certain tinniness told me it was only our
boombox. The bedroom door clicked open. I recog-
nized Matthew's step and pulled the quilt over my
head. He knelt beside the mattress and laid his hand
over my heart; I was forgiven. "I brought you something," he said.

"What?"

"Come out and I'll show you."

I uncovered my head, then yanked the quilt back
up. Matthew was holding an open straight razor two
inches from my face. "Don't you want it?" he asked
innocently.

"Not against my eyeballs."

"Here, I'm taking it away." I felt something long
and narrow being set down on my stomach. I pushed
the quilt away, looked at the razor, touched it with
one finger. Its handle was a smooth curve of ivory,
polished as if it had accustomed itself to a familiar
hand over the years. Its blade gleamed as coldly as
Matthew's smile. "Where did it come from?" I asked.

"What difference does that make? It's yours
now — I even had it sharpened for you. It should cut
beautifully."

"Cut what?"

"Anything you like, Zee. Do you want it or not?"

"Yes. I want anything you give me. It's beautiful.
Thank you."

"I want you to keep it with you always."

"Why?"

"Because I gave it to you. Do you need any other reason?" He stood up and I thought he was going to walk out of the room, but he was unzipping his jeans. He stepped out of them, then slipped his underwear off. "Are you wearing anything under that quilt?" he asked.

"No."

He sat on the edge of the mattress. "Take it off. Let's see."

I untangled myself from the quilt, watching him. His skin looked very pale against the baggy blue T-shirt he still wore. "Sit up," he told me. "Spread your legs. I'm going to watch you, Zee. I want you to touch yourself. Here—" He guided my hand to where he wanted it. "Go on," he said quietly. I began to move my hand. Something uncoiled deep within my belly, like basking snakes coming awake, and began to writhe. Ribbons of liquid warmth slid over my fingers. Through slitted eyes I saw Matthew leaning back against the wall. His knees were drawn up against his chest, his fists pressed against his mouth. Very faintly I heard him say, "Zee," then, "Anthony," but before I could think about that, I felt a little stream of fire crackle and ignite beneath my working fingers. It blazed a path up through me, searing my lungs, scooping out my skull with its radiance. Then Matthew was lying on top of me, kissing my lips and my eyelids, and for a moment all I felt was happiness. Eventually I heard what Matthew was saying to me:

"I'll let you do it, Zee. I'll let you do every bit of it, right up until the end. Until then I'll only watch. You can do everything, my love."

I lay on my back with my eyes closed. Matthew's words confused me. I thought I already *had* done it. I

27

didn't realize until much later that he was talking about killing Anthony LaGuerre.

ભ૪ૹ

It was early evening. Darkness had oozed syruplike across the bedroom window, filling each pane until all six were black. The crystal suncatchers looked dull and leaden. I saw a star kindle close to the horizon. I was alone in the room listening to the Isle of Man CD when Matthew came in. He slipped out of his baggy T-shirt and pulled a black sweater over his head. "Come on—we're going out. Bring the razor I gave you. We have something important to do."

I slid my hand beneath the edge of the mattress and groped for the smooth ivory handle. Anthony LaGuerre's voice filled the room: "Don't come to my house, I won't—" Matthew punched the STOP button and tossed me an enormous green sweater with a hole under one arm. I was still struggling into it when he said, "Hurry up. We have to bring Susan, too."

"Why?"

"I want her to drive. She also has a little pistol she stole from some man. It might be useful."

I followed him downstairs. Susan was in the kitchen watching an ancient color television with rabbit ears instead of cable. Every couple of minutes she would stretch out her foot and kick the side of the box to straighten up the wavering picture. The foil-tipped antennas were drooping, threatening to fall on her the next time she disturbed them. Matthew glided up behind her and bent to speak in her ear.

She jumped, then listened. When he had finished, she bolted upstairs. Matthew took my hand. "Come on. We'll wait for her in the car."

We settled ourselves in the back seat. "Where—" I began to ask. Matthew put his mouth over mine, and the familiar heat began to rise in my stomach. He didn't stop kissing me until Susan came out of the house alone and climbed into the front seat.

"Where are we going?" she asked.

"You'll find out when we get there," Matthew told her.

His arms stayed around me throughout the drive. Now and then he leaned forward and told Susan to take a right or a left. I noticed a police car idling along behind us. The driver's face was obscured by smoke from a thick cigar he held between the first two fingers of his left hand. Susan nearly ran a red light. "*Stop!*" Matthew said, and she stomped the brake, throwing us both against the back of her seat. The policeman glanced at us, then noticed a girl in a short skirt and tight sweater sauntering across the street.

"You need to be more careful than that," Matthew told Susan. "This is important. We can't afford to be stopped because of your negligence." I wouldn't have bet money that Susan knew what "negligence" meant, but she drove more cautiously, listening to Matthew's intermittent directions. In twenty minutes we had left the city center behind. When the houses stopped looking alike, I knew we had left the suburbs too. We drove for a long time on a narrow two-lane road. "Slow down," Matthew said. "What does that mailbox say?"

Susan rolled down her window and peered out. "Box 643," she read.

"This should be it, then. Turn into the driveway, but stop before we get too close to the house."

The wheels sprayed gravel as we swung in. A row of red reflectors flanked the driveway, blinking at us. The driveway went up a small hill, stayed level for a time, then humped its way back down to a small cottage set among a thicket of trees.

"Stop here," Matthew said at the top of the hill. He bent and pulled something out from under the seat, then got out of the car before Susan had turned off the engine. I saw that he was carrying a long thin knife, one that looked as if it had been made for gutting.

"Where are we?" Susan asked.

Matthew's eyes glittered in the cloud-dimmed moonlight filtering through the trees. "This is where Anthony LaGuerre lives."

For a split-second I only wondered how he knew this. Then I remembered the press release the girl at the club had given him, and all the details of the evening fell together: Matthew's excited tension; his evil-looking knife; my straight razor and the pistol Susan was supposed to have. I felt a rush of hot liquid in my throat. "Matthew—"

"What?" His voice was as cold and clear as an icicle.

"Why?—I mean, LaGuerre—I can't—"

"You can, Zee. You can if you trust me, because I promise you that this has to be done. We're not going to *hurt* him, not really. You can do it…" He paused, considered me. "Maybe you won't, though. If that's the way you want it, then wait out here. We'll drive you back into town and drop you off wherever you like. Can you live without me?"

"*No!*" A translucent black veil whispered across my eyes. I groped for Matthew. Susan stared at us, fascinated. Matthew caught me and held my arms.

"Good, Zee. You'll come with us, then. It won't be hard. Not if you love me and Anthony."

I don't love Anthony, I wanted to say. *He's a great singer who writes crappy songs. He should have been born in the seventies, it would have been better for all of us. I only love you.* But I couldn't say a word.

Matthew led us down the sloping driveway to the front door of the cottage. The outer walls of the little building were a patchwork of stone. Fragrant vines crawled up the rough surface, drooped back down under the weight of their own flowers. "A good home for a mage," Matthew said—more to himself than to us, I thought. Then, with no hesitation, he rapped sharply on the door.

There was no response. LaGuerre wasn't home, maybe didn't even live here. I closed my eyes and let myself relax. Then Matthew knocked again and a voice inside the cottage said, "It's open! Come in."

I took out my straight razor and followed Matthew and Susan into the cottage. The front room was sparsely furnished, but every object looked as if it had been carefully selected and well-loved. A battered old piano braced one wall. In the opposite corner sat a wooden rocking chair with a gold-embroidered Indian cushion on its cane seat. LaGuerre or someone else had hung exotic travel posters on the walls: London, Calcutta, Shanghai. Each was a blaze of color that jerked and danced in the corners of my eyes.

The voice called out again. "Nina? I'm on the phone. Be out in a few minutes." This time it was unmistakably the voice of Anthony LaGuerre. Mat-

31

thew pointed at the rocking chair — or, rather, at the telephone extension on the floor beside it. He motioned me forward. I lifted the receiver carefully and heard LaGuerre asking, "How did Callie's play go?"

"Oh, you'd have thought she was on Broadway instead of a kindergarten pageant," said the voice of a young woman. "She took three curtain calls. Went around for days singing her big number to anyone who'd listen. She's your kid, all right." Both of them laughed. I heard a child's voice asking a question in the background, and the young woman said, "Hold on a sec, I'll let her tell you about it herself."

"Daddy?" said a kittenish little voice a few seconds later.

"Hi, Cal. Mommy's been telling me how you were the star of the play."

"Oh, *that*. I didn't sing as good as you, but everybody liked it." The little girl sounded no more than four or five — I didn't think LaGuerre himself was past his mid-twenties — but she spoke precisely, with no trace of baby talk. "I wish you would have come."

"I wish so too, Callie. I had a show of my own to do. I'll be driving up to see you next week, you know."

"I know. Do you want to go to the zoo again?"

"No, the museum." This was some kind of private joke between them, I thought, because the girl went off into wild peals of laughter. When she had calmed down, LaGuerre said, "I need to talk to your mom for just another second. Would you do me a favor and put her on again?"

"Sure. What do you say, daddy?"

"I love you, Callie."

"Love you too." There was the sound of the telephone receiver being dropped onto a table, then a sort of scrambling noise.

"Liane?" said LaGuerre.

"Yeah, sorry." The young woman was back. "Hi, Tony. Callie just tried to push the receiver onto the floor. She likes to watch the cord bounce."

"She's a little devil, huh?"

"Just like her father." The young woman giggled. "Are you still coming up next week?"

Matthew touched my shoulder, surprising me; I had been drawn into the world of the little family. *Liane LaGuerre,* I thought, *what a pretty name that would be, I wonder if they were ever married.* "You've been listening long enough," he mouthed. "Hang up — quietly."

I put the receiver back on the cradle as softly as I could.

"Good. Now stand here beside me." Matthew was trembling. One of his hands touched the small of my back; the other rested on the haft of his knife, which he had tucked into one of his belt loops. I sensed Susan somewhere behind us. She was fidgeting, probably biting her nails. I saw Matthew's chin lift and his eyes narrow. LaGuerre was padding down the hall. His voice reached us before he did. "Hi, Nina. Sorry I took so long. I was talking—" He came into the room and saw us. His mouth stayed open. The pink tip of his tongue darted out to moisten his lips. Finally he said, "Who the hell are *you*?"

Matthew took a step forward. "Don't be afraid, Anthony." LaGuerre's eyes flicked from Matthew's knife to the straight razor in my hand to Susan's pistol, which she was clasping to her chest, the barrel

33

pointed at the underside of her chin. If it had gone off, the bullet would have plowed a dripping furrow through her face.

Matthew went right up to LaGuerre, lowered himself to his knees, and lovingly, with exquisite gentleness, bent to kiss LaGuerre's bare feet. "You are too beautiful for this world," I heard him whisper.

"What —" LaGuerre tried to step back into the hall, but Matthew grasped his ankles. "What do you want?"

"Everything, Anthony. I want everything from you." Matthew stood up again, running his hands along the sides of LaGuerre's body. LaGuerre stood rigidly, too afraid to move, I thought. Matthew brushed a lock of LaGuerre's blonde hair aside and kissed his forehead. Then, in a movement so fast I scarcely saw it, he kicked LaGuerre's feet out from under him and caught him under the arms as he fell. Before LaGuerre could recover enough to struggle, Susan stepped up and pointed the pistol at his head.

"It's all right, Anthony," said Matthew. "Watch out for Susan; she tends to make sudden moves. I want you to lie down on the floor here. Would you like a pillow under your head?" LaGuerre only stared at him. "It will be more comfortable, I think. Zee, do you see a pillow?"

I reached for the Indian cushion on the seat of the rocking chair and handed it to Matthew, who slid it under LaGuerre's head. Then he took the knife out of his belt loop and unzipped his pants. LaGuerre squeezed his eyes shut and moaned.

"Don't be afraid. I'm not going to rape you, not the way you're thinking of. It's your mouth I want,

Anthony. You have a beautiful mouth, did you know that? — so soft and serious. It's the floodgate for that amazing voice of yours. I want to see what else it can do." Matthew smiled, not his usual cold smirk but a wide, cheerful grin. Someone who didn't know him might have thought there was warmth in that grin.

LaGuerre spoke between clenched teeth. "If you think I'll open my mouth for you, you're insane."

"Yes, I probably am. And you *will* open your mouth — I know that. The question is, how strongly will you have to be persuaded?" Matthew ran a finger along LaGuerre's lips. When LaGuerre tried to pull away, Matthew grabbed his chin and held his head immobile. "Zee, give me your razor."

I put it in Matthew's hand. "Take the knife from the floor," he said without looking at me. "You'll need to have something." I bent and picked up the gutting knife. It was light and flexible, but I had no doubt that it was also strong.

LaGuerre tried to catch my eyes. "Please don't do this. There's a phone over by the rocking chair. Call the police. Please, I have a little girl — "

"We know," Matthew said. Just two small words, but the implications of them seemed to horrify LaGuerre into silence. Matthew flicked the razor open, and LaGuerre squeezed his eyes shut again.

"No, Anthony, I want you to see this. Open your eyes." No response. Matthew placed the blade against LaGuerre's cheek. "Please open your eyes now, Anthony." Nothing. Matthew drew the razor down ever so slightly. LaGuerre's eyes flew open, blazing with pain and terror. When Matthew took the blade away there was a thread of blood across LaGuerre's cheek.

"Sharp, you see? Watch this." Matthew pushed up the sleeve of his sweater and drew the blade across his own forearm. A lipless mouth opened, impossibly crimson. I couldn't suppress a tiny moan at the sight, but Matthew never looked at me. He held his arm above LaGuerre's head, letting the drops spatter LaGuerre's pale face. He dipped the tip of his finger in the blood and painted a gaudy red smile on LaGuerre's lips. LaGuerre stared around the room. Our eyes met. At that moment I saw in LaGuerre's eyes that he knew he was going to die tonight. Until now he had hoped we might only rob him, hurt him, humiliate him. Matthew's blood told him the truth.

"Now will you open wide for me, Anthony?"

"You can put your dick in my mouth, but I swear to God I'll bite it off. I don't care what you do to me — you're going to do it anyway. But if you do that, I swear I'll get my teeth in you."

Matthew seemed amused. He stroked LaGuerre's face, ran bloody fingers through LaGuerre's hair. "Not ready to die yet, are you? That could change quickly enough."

"I don't want to die at *all*." Now that he had lost most of his hope, LaGuerre's eyes were furious. "I don't know if I can stop you from killing me, but if you think you're doing me some kind of favor, you can forget that shit right now. *I don't want to die.*"

"Your eyes are sewn shut," Matthew told him. "I'm only cutting them open for you. I want to release you, let your music flow free of a human body's constraints."

"You *are* crazy!" LaGuerre cried. "The music's in *here* — in my brain. You kill me, you're killing that.

36

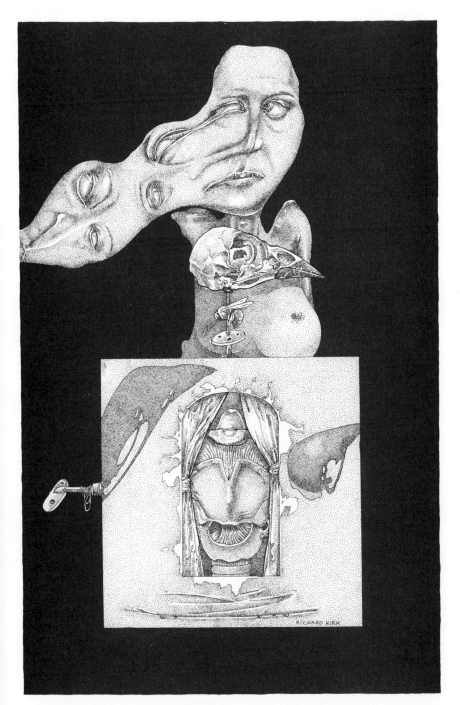

You're..." He let his head fall back against the cushion. "Some kind of devil," he said.

"No, Anthony. I'm not an angel like you, but I'm not a devil either. You and I are brothers, in a way."

"Not...brothers. Not you. You're a destroyer, a...negative space. You're nothing."

The edges of my vision turned to seething sharp-edged red lace. I threw myself at LaGuerre, cracked the flat of my hand across his face, tore at his hair. "You lie! From the minute I heard you, I knew you lied. Matthew is everything in this world. He's everything ever."

LaGuerre seemed to really see me then. "You...were at the show the other night, weren't you? I saw..."

"Yes."

"But..." His eyes were honestly puzzled. "But didn't you *like* it?"

This query struck me as ironically, hysterically funny. I threw my head back and laughed, and Matthew put his mouth close to my ear and said, "Do it now, Zee," so, still laughing as though I might never stop, I lifted Matthew's long thin knife and pushed it into Anthony LaGuerre's stomach. He screamed then, and in his cry I heard all the loneliness I'd known, all the slaps and jabs I'd taken, every hurt that had been unfairly mine. I stabbed him again and screamed with him, into his face. I lay on him and slashed at him and tried to hurt him everywhere. When Matthew pulled me away, I swung at him too. He caught my arm and held it until I collapsed against him.

"Look at Anthony," Matthew told me.

I looked. LaGuerre — no, I could call him Anthony now; I had made him mine — was torn and stained

39

and curled around himself, trying to hold himself in. But he was still alive. He was watching me. The agony in his eyes was tinged with awareness. He still knew what was happening to him. Whatever he had wanted before, all Anthony wanted now was to die. He wanted the pain to be over. "Kill him," I said.

Matthew didn't move. He was watching Anthony, transfixed.

"KILL HIM!" I shrieked.

Matthew started, came out of his fugue, crawled up and eased Anthony's head onto his lap. He bent and spoke: "Bare your throat. It will be over."

Something like relief crossed Anthony's bloody face. He lifted his chin and closed his eyes. Matthew drew the razor in one quick strong swipe across his throat, opening both the jugular and the carotid. A vast red tide poured out, bright oxygen-rich blood and dusky heart's blood swirling together, soaking Matthew's pants. Anthony's eyelids fluttered. His hands knotted into fists, then relaxed. He was gone.

Susan had been standing by the rocking chair, shifting her weight from foot to foot, watching the whole thing. Finally she asked, "Can I stab him once?"

"Shut up," Matthew told her. He kissed Anthony's slack bloody lips. I watched, not jealous, not caring. Matthew got to his feet and nodded at Susan. "Go out and start the car." When she had gone, he took my hand. "Come home with me. I love you more than anything in the world."

The sky had begun to clear. Stars floated in the emptiness, flaring and dwindling between rags of dark gray cloud. In the car, Matthew held his fingers to my lips and forced me to take one into my mouth. I knew the dull coppery taste was Anthony

40

LaGuerre's drying blood. Matthew traced the shape of my eyes with his tongue, bit my throat, pushed me down across the seat and tore at my clothes until I was naked enough to please him. Susan spared us one curious glance in the rearview mirror, then turned her eyes back to the glittering road.

CR80

I lay upstairs on our mattress for days. It might have been weeks. Matthew wouldn't let anybody else into the room. He brought me food, sometimes hot, sometimes cold, which I did not eat unless he fed it to me with a spoon. Sometimes he pushed my knees up to my chest and fucked me. My body responded to this; my mind barely knew it was happening. Once he told me he wouldn't touch me again until I had a bath, so I let him lead me down the hall and soap me clean in the big rust-stained tub that stood on four clawed feet.

In the daytime, I watched the sun splinter through the crystal suncatchers and turn them into points of multicolored fire. At night I stared into the darkness, watching the designs that sparkled and faded there. Once Matthew sat beside me on the mattress and said, "Susan has been bragging to the others about what we did." I shut my eyes. Some time later, he told me that one of the Jennifers and the cokehead guy were gone.

"I love you," he told me over and over. I don't remember whether I said it back to him.

On the last night, I woke wondering why my dreams had flickered so strange and blue across the walls of my skull. Matthew was sitting up with the

41

quilt pooled around his waist, staring at the window. A whirling bubble light swept the room again and again. "THIS IS THE POLICE," an amplified voice told the house. "ALL OCCUPANTS COME OUT WITH YOUR HANDS IN FULL VIEW. REPEAT—"

Far below us, the front door slammed and feet went running down the walk. The night exploded with three sharp cracks, each loud enough to shake the walls. A scream swelled and died—Susan's voice, raised in a last pitiful sound of rage. Something clattered across the concrete walk. Her pistol, I supposed.

I sat up next to Matthew. He pulled the quilt around my shoulders, and we held each other.

"Susan told, you know."

I nodded.

"My knife is gone. Jennifer and what's-his-name must have taken it. If they knew what to do with it, it could prove everything."

"Does it matter?"

"No. We had to do it. I can't be sorry. But they'll kill me, Zee. You know that. I don't want to die for them, *entertaining* them. I'd rather stay here with you."

I looked at him. I couldn't see the expression in his eyes, but the whirling blue light called up sparks from deep within them. I let my eyes trail over the line of his jaw, his chest, the long hump of his legs under the quilt. I thought about what he had just said. He was right; they would kill him, though I wasn't sure how. I imagined the strong body I had loved burning in the electric chair, imagined government-issue poison flowing into the veins of his arm, the veins I had traced with my tongue.

"Lean back against me," I told him.

42

He settled himself between my legs. The back of his head rested against my chest. I slid my hand under the mattress, and for a moment I thought it too was gone; then my fingers touched its smooth ivory curve, the gift Matthew had made me promise to keep forever. He tilted his head back to look at me. His eyes were dark hollows.

"Watch carefully," he said. "My face might change."

The blade went into his throat as easily as a knife sliding through butter. His eyes widened, but he made no sound. The blood washing over my hands felt clean, sticky, no hotter or colder than anyone else's. I bent over him and watched, waiting for the next sweep of blue light, trying to see the change that would come over his face.

When they came to get me, I was still waiting.

Onion

by Caitlín R. Kiernan

Frank was seven years old when he found the fields of red grass growing behind the basement wall. The building on St. Mark's where his parents lived after his father took a job in Manhattan and moved them from the New Jersey suburbs across the wide, gray Hudson. And of course he'd been told to stay out of the basement, no place for a child to play because there were rats down there, his mother said, and rats could give you tetanus and rabies. Rats might even be carrying plague, she said, but the sooty blackness at the foot of the stairs was too much temptation for any seven-year-old, the long, long hallway past the door to the super's apartment and sometimes a single naked bulb burned way down at the end of that hall. Dirty, whiteyellow stain that only seemed to emphasize the gloom, drawing attention to just how very dark dark could be, and after school Frank would stand at the bottom of the stairs for an hour at a time, peering into the hall that led down to the basement.

"Does your mama know you're always hanging around down here?" Mr. Sweeney would ask whenever he came out and found Frank lurking in the shadows. Frank would squint at the flood of light from Mr. Sweeney's open door, would shrug or mumble the most noncommittal response he could come up with.

"I bet you she don't," Mr. Sweeney would say. "I bet she *don't* know."

"Are there really rats down there?" Frank might ask and Mr. Sweeney would nod his head, point towards the long hall and say "You better *believe* there's rats. Boy, there's rats under this dump big as German shepherd puppies. They got eyes like acetylene blow torches and teeth like carving knives. Can chew straight through concrete, these rats we got."

"Then why don't you get a cat?" Frank asked once and Mr. Sweeney laughed, phlegmy old man laugh, and "Oh, we had some cats, boy," he said. "We had whole goddamn cat *armies*, but when these rats get done, ain't never anything left but some gnawed-up bones and whiskers."

"I don't believe that," Frank said. "Rats don't get that big. Rats don't eat cats."

"You better get your skinny rump back upstairs, or they're gonna eat you too," and then Mr. Sweeney laughed again and slammed his door, left Frank alone in the dark, his heart thumping loud and his head filled with visions of the voracious, giant rats that tunneled through masonry and dined on any cat unlucky enough to get in their way.

And that's the way it went, week after week, month after month, until one snowblind February afternoon, too cold and wet to go outside and his mother didn't notice when he slipped quietly downstairs with the flashlight she kept in a kitchen drawer. Mr. Sweeney was busy with a busted radiator on the third floor, so nobody around this time to tell him scary stories and chase him home again, and Frank walked right on past the super's door, stood shivering in the chilly, mildewstinking air of the hallway. The unsteady beam of his flashlight to show narrow walls that might have been blue or green a long time ago, little black-and-white, six-sided ceramic tiles on the floor, but half of them missing and he could see the rotting boards underneath. There were doors along the length of the hall, some of them boarded up, nailed shut, one door frame without any door at all and he stepped very fast past that one.

Indiana Jones wouldn't be afraid, he thought, counting his footsteps in case that might be important later on, listening to the winter wind yowling raw along the street as it swept past the building on its way to Tompkins Square Park and the East River. Twenty steps, twenty-five, thirty-three and then he was standing below the dangling bulb and for the first time Frank stopped and looked back the way he'd come. And maybe he'd counted wrong, because it seemed a lot farther than only thirty-three steps back to the dim and postage-stamp-sized splotch of day at the other end of the hall.

Only ten steps more down to the basement door, heavy, gray steel door with a rusted hasp and a Yale padlock, but standing wide open like it was waiting for him and maybe Mr. Sweeney only forgot to lock it the last time he came down to check the furnace or wrap the pipes. And later, Frank wouldn't remember much about crossing the threshold into the deeper night of the basement, the soupthick stench and taste of dust and rot and mushrooms, picking his way through the maze of sagging shelves and wooden crates, decaying heaps of rags and newspapers, past the ancient furnace crouched in one corner like a cast-iron octopus. Angry, orangered glow from the furnace grate like the eyes of the super's cat-eating rats — he *would* remember that — and then Frank heard the dry, rustling sound coming from one corner of the basement.

Years later, through high school and college and the slow purgatory of his twenties, *this* is where the bad dreams would always begin, the moment that he lifted the flashlight and saw the wide and jagged crack in the concrete wall. A faint draft from that corner that smelled of cinnamon and ammonia, and he *knew* better than to look, knew he should turn and run all the way back because it wasn't ever really rats that he was supposed to be afraid of. The rats just a silly, grown-up lie to keep him safe, smaller, kinder nightmare for his own good, and *Run, boy,* Mr Sweeney whispered inside his head. *Run fast while you still can, while you still don't know.*

But Frank didn't run away, and when he pressed his face to the crack in the wall, he could see that the fields stretched away for miles and miles, crimson meadows beneath a sky the yellowgreen of an old bruise. The white trees that writhed and rustled in the choking, spicy breeze, and far, far away, the black thing striding slowly through the grass on bandy, stiltlong legs.

෬෭

Frank and Willa share the tiny apartment on Mott Street, roachy Chinatown hovel one floor above an apothecary so the place always stinks of ginseng and jasmine and the powdered husks of dried sea creatures. Four walls, a gas range, an ancient Frigidaire that only works when it feels like it, but together they can afford the rent, most of the time, and the month or two they've come up short Mrs. Wu has let them slide. His job at a copy shop and hers waiting tables and sometimes they talk about moving out of the city, packing up their raggedy-ass belongings and riding a Greyhound all the way to Florida, all the way to the Keys, and then it'll be summer all year long. But not this sticky, sweltering New York summer, no, it would be clean ocean air and rum drinks, sunwarm sand and the lullaby roll and crash of waves at night.

Frank is still in bed when Willa comes out of the closet that passes as their bathroom, naked and dripping from the shower, her hair wrapped up in a towel that used to be white and he stops staring at the tattered Cézanne print thumbtacked over the television and stares at her instead. Willa is tall and her skin so pale he thought she might be sick the first time they met, so skinny that he can see intimations of her skeleton beneath that skin like milk and pearls. Can trace the bluegreen network of veins and capillaries in her throat, between her small breasts, winding like hesitant, watercolor brush strokes down her arms. He's pretty sure that one day Willa will finally figure out she can do a hell of lot better than him and move on,

49

but he tries not to let that ruin whatever it is they have now.

"It's all yours," she says, his turn even though the water won't be hot again for at least half an hour, and Willa sits down in a chair near the foot of the bed. She leans forward and rubs vigorously at her hair trapped inside the dingy towel.

"We could both play hooky," Frank suggests hopefully, watching her, imagining how much better sex would be than the chugging, headache drone of Xerox machines, the endless dissatisfaction of clients. "You could come back to bed and we could lie here all day. We could just lie here and sweat and watch television."

"Jesus, Frank, how am I supposed to resist an offer like *that*?"

"Okay, so we could screw and sweat and watch television."

She stops drying her hair and glares at him, shakes her head and frowns, but the sort of frown that says *I wish I could* more than it says anything else.

"That new girl isn't working out," she says.

"The fat chick from Kazakhstan?" Frank asks and he rolls over onto his back, easier to forget the fantasies of a lazy day alone with Willa if he isn't looking at her sitting there naked.

"Fucking *Kazakhstan*. I mean, what the hell were Ted and Daniel thinking? She can't even speak enough English to tell someone where the toilet is, much less take an order."

"Maybe they felt sorry for her," Frank says unhelpfully and now he's staring up at his favorite crack on the waterstained ceiling, the one that always makes him think of a Viking orbiter photo of the Valles Marineris from one of his old astronomy books. "I've heard that people do that sometimes, feel sorry for people."

"Well, they'd probably lose less money if they just sent the bitch to college, the way she's been pissing off customers."

"Maybe you should suggest that today," and a moment later Willa's wet towel smacks him in the face, steamydamp terry cloth that smells like her black hair dye and the cheap baby shampoo she uses. It covers his eyes, obscuring his view of the Martian rift valley overhead, but Frank doesn't move the towel immediately, better to lie there a moment longer, breathing her in.

"Is it still supposed to rain today?" Willa asks and he mumbles through the wet towel that he doesn't know.

"They keep promising it's going to rain and it keeps not raining."

Frank sits up and the towel slides off his face and into his lap, lies there as the dampness begins to soak through his boxers.

"I don't know," he says again; Willa has her back turned to him and she doesn't reply or make any sign to show that she's heard. She's pulling a bright yellow T-shirt on over her head, the Curious George shirt he gave her for Christmas, has put on a pair of yellow panties, too.

"I'm sorry," she says. "It's the heat. The heat's driving me crazy."

Frank glances towards the window, the sash up but the chintzy curtains hanging limp and lifeless in the stagnant July air; he'd have to get out of bed, walk

51

all the way across the room, lean over the sill and peer up past the walls and rooftops to see if there are any clouds. "It might rain today," he says, instead.

"I don't think it's ever going to rain again as long as I live," Willa says and steps into her jeans. "I think we've broken this goddamn planet and it's never going to rain anywhere ever again."

Frank rubs his fingers through his stiff, dirty hair and looks back at the Cézanne still life above the television—a tabletop, the absinthe bottle and a carafe of water, an empty glass, the fruit that might be peaches.

"You'll be at the meeting tonight?" he asks and Frank keeps his eyes on the print because he doesn't like the sullen, secretive expression Willa gets whenever they have to talk about the meetings.

"Yeah," she says, sighs, and then there's the clothmetal sound of her zipper. "Of course I'll be at the meeting. Where the hell else would I be?"

And then she goes back into the bathroom and shuts the door behind her, leaves Frank alone with Cézanne and the exotic reek of the apothecary downstairs, Valles Marineris and the bright day spilling uninvited through the window above Mott Street.

Half past two and Frank sits on a plastic milk crate in the stockroom of Gotham Kwick Kopy, trying to decide whether or not to eat the rest of the peanut butter and honey sandwich he brought for lunch. The air conditioning's on the blink again and he thinks it might actually be hotter inside the shop than out on the street; a few merciful degrees cooler in the stockroom, though, shadowy refuge stacked high with cardboard boxes of copy paper in a dozen shades of white and all the colors of the rainbow. He peels back the top of his sandwich, the doughy Millbrook bread that Willa likes, and frowns at the mess underneath. So hot out front that the peanut butter has melted, oily mess to leak straight through wax paper and the brown bag and he's trying to remember if peanut butter and honey can spoil.

Both the stockroom doors swing open and Frank looks up, blinks and squints at the sunframed silhouette, Joe Manske letting in the heat and "Hey, don't do that," Frank says as Joe switches on the lights. The fluorescents buzz and flicker uncertainly, chasing away the shadows, drenching the stockroom in their bland, indifferent glare.

"Dude, why are you sitting back here in the dark?" Joe asks and for a moment Frank considers throwing the rest of the sandwich at him.

"Why aren't you working on that Mac?" Frank asks right back and "It's fixed, good as new, " Joe says, grins his big, stupid grin, and sits down on a box of laser print paper near the door.

"That fucker won't *ever* be good as new again."

"Well, at least it's stopped making that sound. That's good enough for me," and Joe takes out a pack of Camels, offers one to Frank and Frank shakes his head no. A month now since his last cigarette, quitting because Willa's stepmother is dying of lung cancer, quitting because cigarettes cost too goddamn much, anyhow, and "Thanks, though," he says.

"Whatever," Joe Manske mumbles around the filter of his Camel, thumb on the strike wheel of his silver lighter and in a moment the air is filled with the pungent aroma of burning tobacco. Frank gives up on the dubious sandwich, drops it back into the brown bag and crumples the bag into a greasy ball.

"I fuckin' hate this fuckin' job," Joe says, disgusted, smoky cloud of words about his head, and he points at the stockroom doors with his cigarette. "You just missed a real piece of work, man."

"Yeah?" and Frank tosses the sandwich ball towards the big plastic garbage can sitting a few feet away, misses and it rolls behind the busted Canon 2400 color copier that's been sitting in the same spot since he started this job a year ago.

"Yeah," Joe says. "I was trying to finish that pet store job and this dude comes in, little bitty old man looks like he just got off the boat from Poland or Armenia or some shit—"

"My grandfather was Polish," Frank says and Joe sighs loudly, long impatient sigh and he flicks ash onto the cement floor. "You *know* what I mean."

"So what'd he want, anyway?" Frank asks, not because he cares but the shortest way through any conversation with Joe Manske is usually right down the middle, just be quiet and listen and sooner or later he'll probably come to the end and shut up.

"He had this *old* book with him. The damned thing must have been even older than him and it was falling apart. I don't think you could so much as look at it without the pages crumbling. Had it tied together with some string and he kept askin' me all these questions, real technical shit about the machines, you know."

"Yeah? Like what?"

"Dude, I don't know. I can't remember half of it, techie shit, like I was friggin' Mr. Wizard or somethin'.

54

I finally just told him we couldn't be responsible if the copiers messed up his old book, but he still kept on askin' these questions. Lucky for me, one of the self-service machines jammed and I told him I had to go fix it. By the time I was finished, he was gone."

"You live to serve," Frank says, wondering if Willa would be able to tell if he had just one cigarette. "The customer is always right."

"Fuck that shit," Joe Manske says. "I don't get paid enough to have to listen to some senile old fart jabberin' at me all day."

"Yes sir, helpful is your middle name."

"Fuck you."

Frank laughs and gets up, pushes the milk crate towards the wall with the toe of one shoe so no one's going to come along later and trip over it, break their neck and have him to blame. "I better get back to work," he says and "You do that," Joe grumbles and puffs his Camel.

Through the stockroom doors and back out into the stifling, noisy clutter of the shop, and it must be at least ten degrees warmer out here, he thinks. There's a line at the register and the phone's ringing, no one out front but Maggie and she glowers at him across the chaos. "I'm on it," Frank says; she shakes her head doubtfully and turns to help a woman wearing a dark purple dress and matching beret. Frank's reaching across the counter for the telephone receiver when he notices the business card lying near a display of Liquid Paper. Black sans serif print on an expensive, white cotton card stock and what appears to be an infinity symbol in the lower left-hand corner. FOUND: LOST WORLDS centered at the top, TERRAE NOVUM ET TERRA INDETERMINATA on the next line down

55

in smaller letters. Then a name and an address—Dr. Solomon Monalisa, Ph. D., 43 W. 61st St., Manhattan—but no number or e-mail, and Frank picks up the card, holds it so Maggie can see.

"Where'd this come from?" he asks but she only shrugs, annoyed but still smiling her strained and weary smile for the woman in the purple beret. "Beats me. Ask Joe, if he ever comes back. Now, will you *please* answer the phone?"

He apologizes, lifts the receiver, "Gotham Kwick Kopy, Frank speaking. How may I help you?" and slips the white card into his back pocket.

CRSO

The group meets in the basement of a synagogue on Eldridge Street. Once a month, eight o'clock until everyone who wants to talk has taken his or her turn, coffee and stale doughnuts before and afterwards. Metal folding chairs and a lectern down front, a microphone and crackly PA system even though the room isn't really large enough to need one. Never more than fourteen or fifteen people, occasionally as few as six or seven, and Frank and Willa always sit at the very back, near the door. Sometimes Willa doesn't make it all the way through a meeting and she says she hates the way they all watch her if she gets up to leave early, like she's done something wrong, she says, like this is all her fault, somehow. So they sit by the door, which is fine with Frank; he'd rather not have everyone staring at the back of his head, anyway.

He's sipping at a styrofoam cup of the bitter, black coffee, three sugars and it's still bitter, watching the others, all their familiar, telltale quirks and peculiarities, their equivocal glances, when Willa comes in. First the sound of her clunky motorcycle boots on the concrete steps and then she stands in the doorway a moment, that expression like it's always the first time for her and it can never be any other way.

"Hey," Frank says quietly. "I made it," she replies and sits down beside him. There's a stain on the front of her Curious George T-shirt that looks like chocolate sauce.

"How was your day?" he asks her, talking so she doesn't lock up before things even get started.

"Same as ever. It sucked. They didn't fire Miss Kazakhstan."

"That's good, dear. Would you like a martini?" and he jabs a thumb towards the free-coffee-and-stale-doughnut table. "I think I'll pass," Willa says humorlessly, rubs her hands together and stares at the floor between her feet. "I think my stomach hurts enough already."

"Would you rather just go home? We can miss one night. I sure as hell don't care—"

"*No*," she says, answering too fast, too emphatic, so he knows she means yes. "That would be silly. I'll be fine when things get started."

And then Mr. Zaroba stands, stocky man with skin like tea-stained muslin, salt-and-pepper hair and beard and his bushy, gray eyebrows. Kindly blue grandfather eyes and he raises one hand to get everyone's attention, as if they aren't all looking at him already, as if they haven't all been waiting for him to open his mouth and break the tense, uncertain silence.

"Good evening, everyone," he says, and Willa sits up a little straighter in her chair, expectant arch of her back as though she's getting ready to run.

"Before we begin," Mr. Zaroba continues, "there's something I wanted to share. I came across this last week," and he takes a piece of paper from his shirt pocket, unfolds it, and begins to read. An item from the *New York Tribune*, February 17th, 1901; reports by an Indian tribe in Alaska of a city in the sky that was seen sometimes, and a prospector named Willoughby who claimed to have witnessed the thing himself in 1897, claimed to have tried to photograph it on several occasions and succeeded, finally.

"And now this," Zaroba says and he pulls a second folded sheet of paper from his shirt pocket, presto, bottomless bag of tricks, that pocket, and this time he reads from a book, *Alaska* by Miner Bruce, page 107, he says. Someone else who saw the city suspended in the arctic sky, a Mr. C. W. Thornton of Seattle, and "'It required no effort of the imagination to liken it to a city,'" Mr. Zaroba reads, "'but was so distinct that it required, instead, faith to believe that it was not in reality a city.'"

People shift nervously in their seats, scuff their feet, and someone whispers too loudly.

"I have the prospector's photograph," Zaroba says. "It's only a xerox from the book, of course. It isn't very clear, but I thought some of you might like to see it," and he hands one of the sheets of paper to the person sitting nearest him.

"Damn, I need a cigarette," Willa whispers and "You and me both," Frank whispers back. It takes almost five minutes for the sheet of paper to make its way to the rear of the room, passed along from hand

to hand to hand while Zaroba stands patiently at the front, his head bowed solemn as if leading a prayer. Some hold onto it as long as they dare and others hardly seem to want to touch it. A man three rows in front of them gets up and brings it back to Willa.

"I don't see nothing but clouds," he says, sounding disappointed.

And neither does Frank, fuzzy photograph of a mirage, deceit of sunlight in the collision of warm and freezing air high above a glacier, but Willa must see more. She holds the paper tight and chews at her lower lip, traces the distorted peaks and cumulonimbus towers with the tip of an index finger.

"My god," she whispers.

In a moment Zaroba comes up the aisle and takes the picture away, leaves Willa staring at her empty hands, her eyes wet like she might start crying. Frank puts an arm around her bony shoulders, but she immediately wiggles free and scoots her chair a few inches farther away.

"So, who wants to get us started tonight?" Mr. Zaroba asks when he gets back to the lectern. At first no one moves or speaks or raises a hand, each looking at the others or trying hard to look nowhere at all. And then a young woman stands up, younger than Willa, filthy clothes and bruisedark circles under her eyes, hair that hasn't been combed or washed in ages. Her name is Janice and Frank thinks that she's a junky, probably a heroin addict because she always wears long sleeves.

"Janice? Very good, then," and Mr. Zaroba returns to his seat in the first row. Everyone watches Janice as she walks slowly to the front of the room, or they pretend not to watch her. There's a small hole in the

61

seat of her dirty, threadbare jeans and Frank can see that she isn't wearing underwear. She stands behind the lectern, coughs once, twice, and brushes her shaggy bangs out of her face. She looks anxiously at Mr. Zaroba and "It's all right, Janice," he says. "Take all the time you need. No one's going to rush you."

"Bullshit," Willa mutters, loud enough that the man sitting three rows in front of them turns and scowls. "What the hell are you staring at," she growls and he turns back towards the lectern.

"It's okay, baby," Frank says and takes her hand, squeezes hard enough that she can't shake him loose this time. "We can leave anytime you want."

Janice coughs again and there's a faint feedback whine from the mike. She wipes her nose with the back of her hand and "I was only fourteen years old," she begins. "I still lived with my foster parents in Trenton and there was this old cemetery near our house, Riverview Cemetery. Me and my sister, my foster sister, we used to go there to smoke and talk, you know, just to get away from the house."

Janice looks at the basement ceiling while she speaks, or down at the lectern, but never at the others. She pauses and wipes her nose again.

"We went there all the time. Wasn't anything out there to be afraid of, not like at home. Just dead people, and me and Nadine weren't afraid of dead people. Dead people don't hurt anyone, right? We could sit there under the trees in the summer and it was almost like things weren't so bad. Nadine was a year older than me."

Willa tries to pull her hand free, digs her nails into Frank's palm but he doesn't let go. They both know where this is going, have both heard Janice's story so many times they could recite it backwards, same tired old horror story, and "It's okay," he says out loud, to Willa or to himself.

"Mostly it was just regular headstones, but there were a few big crypts set way back near the water. I didn't like being around them. I told her that, over and over, but Nadine said they were like little castles, like something out of fairy tales.

"One day one of them was open, like maybe someone had busted into it, and Nadine had to see if there were still bones inside. I begged her not to, said whoever broke it open might still be hanging around somewhere and we ought to go home and come back later. But she wouldn't listen to me.

"I didn't want to look inside. I swear to God, I didn't."

"*Liar,*" Willa whispers, so low now that the man three rows in front of them doesn't hear, but Frank does. Her nails are digging deeper into his palm, and his eyes are beginning to water from the pain. "*You* wanted to see," she says. "Just like the rest of us, you wanted to see."

"I said, 'What if someone's still in there?' but she wouldn't listen. She wasn't ever afraid of anything. She used to lay down on train tracks just to piss me off."

"What did you see in the crypt, Janice, when you and Nadine looked inside?" Mr. Zaroba asks, but no hint of impatience in his voice, not hurrying her or prompting, only helping her find a path across the words as though they were slippery rocks in a cold stream. "Can you tell us?"

Janice takes a very deep breath, swallows, and "Stairs," she says. "Stairs going down into the ground.

63

There was a light way down at the bottom, a blue light, like a cop car light. Only it wasn't flashing. And we could hear something moving around down there, and something else that sounded like a dog panting. I tried to get Nadine to come back to the house with me then, but she wouldn't. She said 'Those stairs might go *anywhere*, Jan. Don't you want to *see*? Don't you want to *know*?'"

Another pause and "I couldn't stop her," Janice says.

Willa mutters something Frank doesn't understand, then, something vicious, and he lets go of her hand, rubs at the four crescent-shaped wounds her nails leave behind. Blood drawn, crimson tattoos to mark the wild and irreparable tear in her soul by marking him, and he presses his palm to his black work pants, no matter if it stains, no one will ever notice.

"I waited at the top of the stairs until dark," Janice says. "I kept on calling her. I called her until my throat hurt. When the sun started going down, the blue light at the bottom got brighter and once or twice I thought I could see someone moving around down there, someone standing between me and the light. Finally, I yelled I was going to get the goddamn cops if she didn't come back…" and Janice trails off, hugs herself like she's cold and gazes straight ahead, but Frank knows she doesn't see any of them sitting there, watching her, waiting for the next word, waiting for *their* turns at the lectern.

"You don't have to say any more tonight," Zaroba says. "You know we'll all understand if you can't."

64

"No," Janice says. "I *can*...I really *need* to," and she squeezes her eyes shut tight. Mr. Zaroba stands, takes one reassuring step towards the lectern.

"We're all right here," he says, and "We're *listening*," Willa mumbles mockingly. "We're listening," Zaroba says a second later.

"I didn't go get the police. I didn't tell anyone anything until the next day. My foster parents, they just thought she'd run away again. No one would believe me when I told them about the crypt, when I told them where Nadine had really gone. Finally, they made me show them, though, the cops did, so I took them out to Riverview."

"Why do we always have to fucking start with her?" Willa whispers. "I can't remember a single time she didn't go first."

Someone sneezes and "It was sealed up again," Janice says, her small and brittle voice made big and brittle by the PA speakers. "But they opened it. The cemetery people didn't want them to, but they did anyway. I swore I'd kill myself if they didn't open it and get Nadine out of there."

"Can *you* remember a time she didn't go first?" Willa asks and Frank looks at her, but he doesn't answer.

"All they found inside was a coffin. The cops even pulled up part of the marble floor, but there wasn't anything under it, just dirt."

A few more minutes, a few more details, and Janice is done. Mr. Zaroba hugs her and she goes back to her seat. "Who wants to be next?" he asks them and it's the man who calls himself Charlie Jones, though they all know that's not his real name. Every month he apologizes because he can't use his real

65

name at the meetings, too afraid someone at work might find out, and then he tells them about the time he opened a bedroom door in his house in Hartford and there was nothing on the other side but stars. When he's done, Zaroba shakes his hand, pats him on the back, and now it's time for the woman who got lost once on the subway, two hours just to get from South Ferry to the Houston Street Station, alone in an empty train that rushed along through a darkness filled with the sound of children crying. Then a timid Colombian woman named Juanita Lazarte, the night she watched two moons cross the sky above Peekskill, the morning the sun rose in the south.

And all the others, each in his or her turn, as the big wall clock behind the lectern ticks and the night fills up with the weight and absurdity of their stories, glimpses of impossible geographies, entire worlds hidden in plain view if you're unlucky enough to see them. "If you're damned," Juanita Lazarte once said and quickly crossed herself. Mr. Zaroba there whenever anyone locks up, his blue eyes and gentle ministrations, Zaroba who was once an atmospheric scientist and pilot for the Navy. He's seen something too, of course, the summer of 1969, flying supplies in a Hercules C-130 from Christchurch, New Zealand to McMurdo Station. A freak storm, whiteout conditions and instrument malfunction, and when they finally found a break in the clouds somewhere over the Transantarctic Mountains the entire crew saw the ruins of a vast city, glittering obsidian towers and shattered, crystal spires, crumbling walls carved from the mountains themselves. At least that's what Zaroba says. He also says the Navy pressured the other men into signing papers agreeing never to talk about the flight and when he refused, he was pronounced mentally unsound by a military psychiatrist and discharged.

When Willa's turn comes, she glances at Frank, not a word but all the terrible things right there in her eyes for him to see, unspoken resignation, surrender, and then she goes down the aisle and stands behind the lectern.

CRBO

Frank wakes up from a dream of rain and thunder and Willa's sitting crosslegged at the foot of their bed, nothing on but her pajama bottoms, watching television with the sound off and smoking a cigarette. "Where the hell'd you get that?" he asks, blinks sleepily and points at the cigarette.

"I bought a pack on my break today," she replies, not taking her eyes off the screen. She takes a long drag and the smoke leaks slowly from her nostrils.

"I thought we had an agreement."

"I'm sorry," but she doesn't sound sorry at all, and Frank sits up and blinks at the TV screen, rubs his eyes, and now he can see it's Jimmy Stewart and Katharine Hepburn, *The Philadelphia Story*.

"You can turn the sound up, if you want to," he says. "It won't bother me."

"No, that's okay. I know it by heart, anyway."

And then neither of them says anything else for a few minutes, sit watching the television, and when Willa has smoked the cigarette down to the filter she stubs it out in a saucer.

"I don't think I want to go to the meetings any-more," she says. "I think they're only making it worse for me."

Frank waits a moment before he replies, waiting to be sure that she's finished, and then, "That's your decision, Willa. If that's what you want."

"Of course it's my decision."

"You know what I meant."

"I can't keep reciting it over and over like the rest of you. There's no fucking point. I could talk about it from now till doomsday and it still wouldn't make sense and I'd still be afraid. Nothing Zaroba and that bunch of freaks has to say is going to change that, Frank."

Willa picks up the pack of Camels off the bed, lights another cigarette with a disposable lighter that looks pink by the flickering, grainy light from the TV screen.

"I'm sorry," Frank says.

"Does it help you?" she asks and now there's an angrysharp edge in her voice, Willa's switchblade mood swings, sullen to pissed in the space between heartbeats. "Has it *ever* helped you at all?"

Frank doesn't want to fight with her tonight, wants to close his eyes and slip back down to sleep, back to his raincool dreams. Too hot for an argument, and "I don't know," he says, and that's almost not a lie.

"Yeah, well, whatever," Willa mumbles and takes another drag off her cigarette.

"We'll talk about it in the morning if you want," Frank says and he lies back down, turns to face the open window and the noise of Mott Street at two a.m., the blinking orange neon from a noodle shop across the street.

"I'm not going to change my mind, if that's what you mean," Willa says.

"You can turn the sound up," Frank tells her again and concentrates on the soothing rhythm of the noodle shop sign, orange pulse like campfire light, much, much better than counting imaginary sheep. In a moment he's almost asleep again, scant inches from sleep, and "Did you ever see *Return to Oz*?" Willa asks him.

"What?"

"*Return to Oz*, the one where Fairuza Balk plays Dorothy and Laurie Piper plays Auntie Em."

"No," Frank replies. "I never did," and he rolls over onto his back and stares at the ceiling instead of the neon sign. In the dark and the gray light from the television, his favorite crack looks even more like the Valles Marineris.

"It wasn't anything like *The Wizard of Oz*. I was just a little kid, but I remember it. It scared the hell out of me."

"Your mother let you see scary movies when you were a little kid?"

Willa ignores the question, her eyes still fixed on *The Philadelphia Story* if they're fixed anywhere, and she exhales a cloud of smoke that swirls and drifts about above the bed.

"When the film begins, Auntie Em and Uncle Henry think Dorothy's sick," she says. "They think she's crazy, because she talks about Oz all the time, because she won't believe it was only a nightmare. They finally send her off to a sanitarium for electric shock treatment—"

69

"Jesus," Frank says, not entirely sure that Willa isn't making all this up. "That's horrible."

"Yeah, but it's true, isn't it? It's what really happens to little girls who see places that aren't supposed to be there. People aren't ever so glad you didn't die in a twister that they want to listen to crazy shit about talking scarecrows and emerald cities."

And Frank doesn't answer because he knows he isn't supposed to, knows that she would rather he didn't even try, so he sweats and stares at his surrogate, plaster Mars instead, at the shadow play from the television screen; she doesn't say anything else, and in a little while more, he's asleep.

ॐ

In this dream there is still thunder, no rain from the ocher sky but the crack and rumble of thunder so loud that the air shimmers and could splinter like ice. The tall red grass almost as high as his waist, rippling gently in the wind, and Frank wishes that Willa wouldn't get so close to the fleshy, white trees. She thinks they might have fruit, peaches and she's never eaten a white peach before, she said. Giants fighting in the sky and Willa picking up windfall fruit from the rocky ground beneath the trees; Frank looks over his shoulder, back towards the fissure in the basement wall, back the way they came, but it's vanished.

I should be sacred, he thinks. *No, I should be* scared.

And now Willa is coming back towards him through the crimson waves of grass, her skirt for a linen basket to hold all the pale fruit she's gathered. She's smiling and he tries to remember the last time he saw her smile, *really* smile, not just a smirk or a sneer. She smiles and steps through the murmuring grass that seems to part to let her pass, her bare arms and legs safe from the blades grown sharp as straight razors.

"They *are* peaches," she beams.

But the fruit is the color of school-room chalk, its skin smooth and slick and glistening with tiny, pin-head beads of nectar seeping out through minute pores. "Take one," she says, but his stomach lurches and rolls at the thought, loathe to even touch one of the things and then she sighs and dumps them all into the grass at his feet.

"I used to know a story about peaches," Willa says. "It was a Japanese story, I think. Or maybe it was Chinese."

"I'm pretty sure those *aren't* peaches," Frank says, and he takes a step backwards, away from the pile of sweating, albino fruit.

"I heard the pits are poisonous," she says. "Arsenic, or maybe it's cyanide."

A brilliant flash of chartreuse lightning then and the sky sizzles and smells like charred meat. Willa bends and retrieves a piece of the fruit, takes a bite before he can stop her; the sound of her teeth sinking through its skin, tearing through the colorless pulp inside, is louder than the thunder, and milky juice rolls down her chin and stains her Curious George T-shirt. Something wriggles from between her lips, falls to the grass, and when Willa opens her jaws wide to take another bite Frank can see that her mouth is filled with wriggling things.

"They have to be careful you don't swallow your tongue," she says, mumbling around the white peach. "If you swallow your tongue you'll choke to death."

71

Frank snatches the fruit away from her, grabs it quick before she puts any more of it in her belly, and she frowns and wipes the juice staining her hands off onto her skirt. The half-eaten thing feels warm and he tosses it away.

"Jesus, that was fucking silly, Frank. The harm's already done, *you* know that. The harm was done the day you looked through that hole in the wall."

And then the sky booms its symphony of gangrene and sepsis and lightning stabs down at the world with electric claws, thunder then lightning but that's only the wrong way round if he pretends Willa isn't right, if he pretends that he's seven again and this time he doesn't take the flashlight from the kitchen drawer. This time he does what his mother says and doesn't go sneaking off the minute she turns her back.

Frank stands alone beneath the restless trees, his aching, dizzy head too full of all the time that can't be redeemed, now or then or ever, and he watches as Willa walks alone across the red fields towards the endless deserts of scrap iron and bone, towards the bloated, scarletpurple sun. The black things have noticed her and creep along close behind, stalking silent on ebony, mantis legs.

This time, he wakes up before they catch her.

രജ൬

The long weekend, then, hotter and drier, the sky more white than blue and the air on Mott Street and everywhere else that Frank has any reason to go has grown so ripe, so redolent, that sometimes he pulls the collars of his T-shirts up over his mouth and nose, breathes through the cotton like a surgeon or a wild west bandit, but the smell always gets through anyway. On the news there are people dying of heat stroke and dehydration, people dying in the streets and ERs, but fresh-faced weathermen still promise that it will rain very soon. He's stopped believing them and maybe that means that Willa's right and it never will rain again.

Frank hasn't shown the white card — FOUND: LOST WORLDS — to Willa, keeps it hidden in his wallet, only taking it out when he's alone and no one will see, no one to ask where or what or who. He's read it over and over again, has each line committed to memory, and Monday morning he almost calls Mr. Zaroba about it. The half hour between Willa leaving for the cafe and the time that he has to leave for the copy shop if he isn't going to be late, and he holds the telephone receiver and stares at Dr. Solomon Monalisa's card lying there on the table in front of him. The sound of his heart, the dial-tone drone, and the traffic down on Mott Street, the spice-and-dried-fish odor of the apothecary leaking up through the floorboards, and a fat drop of sweat slides down his forehead and spreads itself painfully across his left eyeball. By the time he's finished rubbing at his eye, calling Zaroba no longer seems like such a good idea after all, and Frank puts the white card back into his wallet, slips it in safe between his driver's license and a dog-eared, expired MetroCard.

Instead he calls in sick, gets Maggie and she doesn't believe for one moment that there's anything at all wrong with him.

"I fucking swear, I can't even get up off the toilet long enough to make a phone call. I'm calling *you* from the head," only half an effort at sounding sincere because they both know this is only going through the motions.

"As we speak—" he starts, but Maggie cuts him off.

"That's enough, Frank. But I'm telling you, man, if you wanna keep this job, you better get your slacker ass down here tomorrow morning."

"Right," Frank says. "I hear you," and she hangs up first.

And then Frank stares at the open window, the sun beating down like the Voice of God out there, and it takes him almost five minutes to remember where to find the next number he has to call.

CRÆÐ

Sidney McAvoy stopped coming to the meetings at the synagogue on Eldridge Street almost a year ago, not long after Frank's first time. Small, hawk-nosed man with nervous, ferrety eyes, and he's always reminded Frank a little of Dustin Hoffman in *Papillon*. Some sort of tension or wound between Sidney and Mr. Zaroba that Frank never fully understood, but he saw it from the start, the way their eyes never met and Sidney never took his turn at the lectern, sat silent, brooding, chewing the stem of a cheap, unlit pipe. And then an argument after one of the meetings, the same night that Zaroba told Janice that she shouldn't ever go back to the cemetery in Trenton, that she should never try to find the staircase and the blue light again. Both men speaking in urgent, angry whispers, Zaroba looking up occasionally to smile a sheepish, embarrassed, apologetic

74

smile. Everyone pretending not to see or hear, talking among themselves, occupied with their stale doughnuts and tiny packets of non-dairy creamer, and then Sidney McAvoy left and never came back.

Frank would've forgotten all about him, almost had forgotten, and then one night he and Willa were coming home late from a bar where they drink sometimes, whenever they're feeling irresponsible enough to spend money on booze. Cheap vodka or cheaper beer, a few hours wasted just trying to feel like everyone else, the way they imagined other, normal people might feel, and they ran into Sidney McAvoy a few blocks from their apartment. He was wearing a ratty green raincoat, even though it wasn't raining, and chewing on one of his pipes, carrying a large box wrapped in white butcher's paper, tied up tight and neat with twine.

"Shit," Willa whispered. "Make like you don't see him," but Sidney had already noticed them and he was busy clumsily trying to hide the big package behind his back.

"I *know* you two," he declared, talking loudly, a suspicious, accusatory glint to his quavering voice. "You're both with Zaroba, aren't you? You still go to his *meetings*." That last word a sneer and he pointed a short, grubby finger at the center of Frank's chest.

"That's really none of your goddamn business, is it?" Willa growled and Frank stepped quickly between them; she mumbled and spit curses behind his back and Sidney McAvoy glared up at Frank with his beadydark eyes. A whole lifetime's worth of bitterness and distrust trapped inside those eyes, eyes that have seen far too much or far too little, and "How have you been, Mr. McAvoy," Frank said, straining to sound friendly, and he managed the sickly ghost of a smile.

Sidney grunted and almost dropped his carefully-wrapped package.

"If you *care* about that girl there," he said, speaking around the stem of the pipe clenched between his yellowed teeth, "you'll keep her away from Zaroba. And you'll both stop *telling* him things, if you know what's good for you. There are more useful answers in a road atlas than you're ever going to get out of that old phony."

"What makes you say that?" Frank asked. "What were you guys fighting about?" but Sidney was already scuttling away down Canal Street, his white package hugged close to his chest. He turned a corner without looking back and was gone.

"Fucking nut job," Willa mumbled. "What the hell's his problem, anyway?"

"Maybe the less we know about him the better," Frank said and he put an arm around Willa's small waist, holding her close to him, trying hard not to think about what could have been in the box but unable to think of anything else.

And two weeks later, dim and snowy last day before Thanksgiving, Frank found Sidney McAvoy's number in the phone book and called him.

ᬊᬊ

A wet comb through his hair, cleaner shirt and socks, and Frank goes out into the sizzling day; across Columbus Park to the Canal Street Station and he takes the M to Grand Street, rides the B line all the way to the subway stop beneath the Museum of Natural History. Rumbling along through the honey-combed earth, the diesel and dust and garbage-scented darkness and him swaddled inside steel and unsteady fluorescent light. Time to think that he'd rather not have, unwelcome luxury of second thoughts, and when the train finally reaches the museum he's almost ready to turn right around and head back downtown. Almost, but Dr. Solomon Monalisa's card is in his wallet to keep him moving, get him off the train and up the concrete steps to the museum entrance. Ten dollars he can't spare to get inside, but Sidney McAvoy will never agree to meet him anywhere outside, too paranoid for a walk in Central Park or a quiet booth in a deli or a coffee shop somewhere.

"People are always listening," he says, whenever Frank has suggested or asked that they meet somewhere without an entrance fee. "You never know what they might overhear."

So sometimes it's the long marble bench in front of the *Apatosaurus*, or the abyssal, blueblack gloom of the Hall of Fishes, seats beneath a planetarium constellation sky, whichever spot happens to strike Sidney's fancy that particular day. His fancy or his cabalistic fantasies, if there's any difference, and today Frank finds him in the Hall of Asiatic Mammals, short and rumpled man in a threadbare tweed jacket and red tennis shoes standing alone before the Indian Leopard diorama, gazing intently in at the pocket of counterfeit jungle and the taxidermied cats. Frank waits behind him for a minute or two, waiting to be noticed, and when Sidney looks up and speaks, he speaks to Frank's reflection.

"I'm very busy today," he says, brusque, impatient. "I hope this isn't going to take long."

And no, Frank says, it won't take long at all, I promise, but Sidney's doubtful expression to show just how much he believes that. He sighs and looks back to the stuffed leopards, papier-mâché trees and wax leaves, a painted flock of peafowl rising to hang forever beneath a painted forest canopy. Snapshot moment of another world and the walls of the dimly-lit hall lined with a dozen or more such scenes.

"You want to know about Monalisa," Sidney says. "That's why you came here, because you think I can tell you who he is."

"Yeah," and Frank reaches into his pocket for his wallet. "He came into the place where I work last week and left this." He takes out the card and Sidney turns around only long enough to get it from him.

"So, you talked to him?"

"No, I didn't. I was eating my lunch in the stock-room when he came in. I didn't actually see him for myself."

Sidney stares at the card, seems to read it care-fully three or four times and then he hands it back to Frank, goes back to staring at the leopards.

"Why didn't you show this to Zaroba?" he asks sarcastically, taunting, but Frank answers him any-way, not in the mood today for Sidney's grudges and intrigues.

"Because I didn't think he'd tell me anything. You know he's more interested in the mysteries than ever finding answers." And Frank pauses, silent for a moment and Sidney's silent, too, both men watching the big cats now — glass eyes, freeze-frame talons, and taut, spectacled haunches — as though the leopards might suddenly spring towards them, all this still-ness just a clever ruse for the tourists and the kiddies;

maybe dead leopards know the nervous, wary faces of men who have seen things that they never should have seen.

"He knows the truth would swallow him whole," Sidney says. The leopards don't pounce and he adds, "He knows he's a coward."

"So who is Dr. Monalisa?"

"A bit of something the truth already swallowed and spat back up," and Sidney chuckles sourly to himself and produces one of his pipes from a jacket pocket. "He's a navigator, a pilot, a cartographer..."

Frank notices that one of the two leopards has captured a stuffed peacock, holds it fast between velvet, razored paws, and he can't remember if it was that way only a moment before.

"He draws maps," Sidney says. "He catalogs doors and windows and culverts."

"That's bullshit," Frank whispers, his voice low now so the old woman staring in at the Giant Panda exhibit won't hear him. "You're trying to tell me he can *find* places?"

"He isn't a sane man, Frank," Sidney says and now he holds up his left hand and presses his palm firmly against the glass, as if he's testing the invisible barrier, gauging its integrity. "He has answers, but he has prices, too. You think *this* is Hell, you see how it feels to be in debt to Dr. Solomon Monalisa."

"It isn't me. It's Willa. I think she's starting to lose it."

"We all lost 'it' a long time ago, Frank."

"I'm afraid she's going to do something. I'm afraid she'll hurt herself."

And Sidney turns his back on the leopards then, takes the pipe from his mouth, and glares up at Frank.

79

But some of the anger, some of the bitterness has gone from his eyes, and "He *might* keep her alive," he says, "but you wouldn't want her back when he was done. If she'd even *come* back. No, Frank. You two stay away from Monalisa. Look for your own answers. You don't think you found that card by accident, do you? You don't really think there are such things as coincidences? That's not even his real address—"

"She can't sleep anymore," Frank says, but now Sidney McAvoy isn't listening, glances back over his shoulder at the Indian rain forest, incandescent daylight, illusory distances, and "I have to go now," he says. "I'm very busy today."

"I think she's fucking *dying*, man," Franks says as Sidney straightens his tie and puts the pipe back into his pocket; the old woman looks up from the panda in its unreal bamboo thicket and frowns at them both.

"I'm very busy today, Frank. Call me next week. I think I can meet you at the Guggenheim next week."

And he walks quickly away towards the Roosevelt Rotunda, past the Siberian Tiger and the Sumatran Rhinoceros, leaving Frank alone with the frowning woman. When Sidney has vanished into the shadows behind a small herd of Indian Elephants, Frank turns back to the leopards and the smudgy hand print Sidney McAvoy has left on their glass.

 CA୫ଌ

Hours and hours later, past sunset to the other side of the wasted day, the night that seems even hotter than the scorching afternoon, and Frank is dreaming that the crack in the basement wall on St. Mark's Place is much too narrow for him to squeeze through. Maybe the way it really happened after all, and then he hears a small, anguished sound from somewhere close behind him, something hurting or lost, and when he turns to see, Frank opens his eyes and there's only the tangerine glow of the noodle shop sign outside the apartment window. He blinks once, twice, but this stubborn world doesn't go away, doesn't break apart into random, kaleidoscopic shards to become some other place entirely. So he sits up, head full of the familiar disappointment, this incontestable solidity, and it takes him a moment to realize that Willa isn't in bed. Faint outline of her body left in the wrinkled sheets and the bathroom light is burning, the door open, so she's probably just taking a piss.

"You okay in there?" he asks, but no reply. The soft drip, drip, drip of the kitchenette faucet, tick of the wind-up alarm clock on the table next to Willa's side of the bed, street noise, but no answer. "Did you fall in or something?" he shouts. "Did you drown?"

And still no response, but his senses waking up, picking out more than the ordinary, everynight sounds, a trilling whine pitched so high he feels it more than hears it, and now he notices the way that the air in the apartment smells.

Go back to sleep, he thinks, but both legs already over the edge of the bed, both feet already on the dusty floor. *When you wake up again it'll be over.*

The trill worming its way beneath his skin, soaking in, pricking gently at the hairs on his arms and the back of his neck, and all the silver fillings in his teeth have begun to hum along sympathetically.

81

Where he's standing, Frank can see into the bathroom, just barely, a narrow slice of linoleum, slice of porcelain toilet tank, a mildew and polyurethane fold of shower curtain. And he thinks that the air has started to shimmer, an almost imperceptible warping of the light escaping from the open door, but that might only be his imagination. He takes one small step towards the foot of the bed and there's Willa, standing naked before the tiny mirror above the bathroom sink. The jut of her shoulder blades and hip bones, the anorexic swell of her rib cage, all the minute details of her painful thinness seem even more pronounced in the harsh and curving light.

"Hey. Is something wrong? Are you sick?" and she turns her head slowly to look at him, or maybe only looking towards him because there's nothing much like recognition on her face. Her wide, unblinking eyes, blind woman's stare, and "Can't you hear me, Willa?" he asks as she turns slowly back to the mirror. Her lips move, shaping rough, inaudible words.

The trilling grows infinitesimally louder, climbs another half-octave, and there's a warm, wet trickle across Frank's lips and he realizes that his nose is bleeding.

Behind Willa the bathroom wall, the shower, the low ceiling — everything — ripples and dissolves and there's a sudden, staccato *pop* as the bulb above the sink blows. And after an instant of perfect darkness, perfect nothing, dull and yellowgreen shafts of light from somewhere far, far above, flickering light from an alien sun shining down through the waters of an alien sea; dim, translucent shapes dart and flash through those depths, bodies more insubstantial than jellyfish, more sinuous than eels, and Willa rises to meet them, arms outstretched, her hair drifting about her face like a halo of seaweed and algae. In the ocean-filtered light, Willa's pale skin seems sleek and smooth as dolphinflesh. Air rushes from her lips, her nostrils, and flows eagerly away in a glassy swirl of bubbles.

The trilling has filled Frank's head so full, and his aching skull, his brain, seem only an instant from merciful implosion, fragile, eggshell bone collapsed by the terrible, lonely sound and the weight of all that water stacked above him. He staggers, takes a step backwards, and now Willa's face is turned up to meet the sunlight streaming down, and she's more beautiful than anyone or anything he's ever seen or dreamt.

Down on Mott Street, the screech of tires, the angry blat of a car horn and someone begins shouting very loudly in Chinese.

And now the bathroom is only a bathroom again, and Willa lies in a limp, strangling heap on the floor, her wet hair and skin glistening in the light from the bulb above the sink. The water rolls off her back, her thighs, spreads across the floor in a widening puddle, and Frank realizes that the trilling has finally stopped, only the memory of it left in his ringing ears and bleeding nose. When the dizziness has passed, he goes to her, sits down on the wet floor and holds her while she coughs and pukes up gouts of salt water and snotty strands of something the color of verdigris. Her skin so cold it hurts to touch, cold coming off her like a fever, and something small and chitinous slips from her hair and scuttles away behind the toilet on long, jointed legs.

"Did you *see*?" she asks him, desperate, rheumy words gurgling out with all the water that she's swallowed. "Did you, Frank? Did you *see* it?"

"Yes," he tells her, just like every time before. "Yes, baby. I did. I saw it all," and Willa smiles, closes her eyes, and in a little while she's asleep. He carries her, dripping, back to their bed and holds her until the sun rises and she's warm again.

CRSO

The next day neither of them goes to work, and some small, niggling part of Frank manages to worry about what will happen to them if he loses the shit job at Gotham Kwick Kopy, if Willa gets fired from the cafe, obstinate shred of himself still capable of caring about such things. How the rent will be paid, how they'll eat, everything that hasn't really seemed to matter in more years than he wants to count. Half the morning in bed and his nosebleed keeps coming back, a roll of toilet paper and then one of their towels stained all the shades of dried and drying blood; Willa wearing her winter coat despite the heat, and she keeps trying to get him to go to a doctor, but no, he says. That might lead to questions, and besides, it'll stop sooner or later. It's always stopped before.

By twelve o'clock, Willa's traded the coat for her pink cardigan, feels good enough that she makes them peanut butter and grape jelly sandwiches, black coffee and stale potato chips, and after he eats Frank begins to feel better, too. But going to the park is Willa's idea, because the apartment still smells faintly of silt and dead fish, muddy, low-tide stink that'll take hours more to disappear completely. He knows the

84

odor makes her nervous, so he agrees, even though he'd rather spend the afternoon sleeping off his headache. Maybe a cold shower, another cup of Willa's bitterstrong coffee, and if he's lucky he could doze for hours without dreaming.

They take the subway up to Fifth, follow the eastern edge of the park north, past the zoo and East Green all the way to Pilgrim Hill and the Conservatory Pond. It's not so very hot that there aren't a few model sailing ships on the pond, just enough breeze to keep their miniature Bermuda sails standing tall and taut as shark fins. Frank and Willa sit in the shade near the Alice in Wonderland statue, her favorite spot in all of Central Park, rocky place near the tea party, granite and rustling leaves, the clean laughter of children climbing about on the huge, bronze mushrooms. A little girl with frizzy black hair and red and white peppermint-striped tights is petting the kitten in Alice's lap, stroking its metal fur and meowling loudly, and "I can't ever remember her name," Willa says.

"What?" Frank asks. "Whose name?" not sure if she means the little girl or the kitten or something else entirely.

"Alice's kitten. I know it had a name, but I never can remember it."

Frank watches the little girl for a moment, and "Dinah," he says. "I think the kitten's name was Dinah."

"Oh, yeah, Dinah. That's it," and he knows that she's just thinking out loud, whatever comes to mind so that she won't have to talk about last night, so the conversation won't accidentally find its own way back to those few drowning moments of chartreuse light and eel shadows. Trying so hard to pretend and he almost decides they're both better off if he plays along and doesn't show her Dr. Solomon Monalisa's white calling card.

"That's a good name for a cat," she says. "If we ever get a kitten, I think I'll name it Dinah."

"Mrs. Wu doesn't like cats."

"Well, we're not going to spend the rest of our lives in that dump. Next time, we'll get an apartment that allows cats."

Frank takes the card out and lays his wallet on the grass, but Willa hasn't even noticed, too busy watching the children clambering about on Alice, too busy dreaming about kittens. The card is creased and smudged from a week riding around in his back pocket and all the handling it's suffered, the edges beginning to fray, and he gives it to her without any explanation.

"What's this?" she asks and he tells her to read it first, just read it, so she does. Reads it two or three times and then Willa returns the card, goes back to watching the children. But her expression has changed, the labored, make-believe smile gone and now she just looks like herself again, plain old Willa, the distance in her eyes, the hard angles at the corners of her mouth that aren't quite a frown.

"Sidney says he's for real," half the truth, at best, and Frank glances down at the card, reading it again for the hundredth or two-hundredth time.

"Sidney McAvoy's a fucking lunatic."

"He says this guy has maps—"

"Christ, Frank. What do you want me to say? You want me to give you *permission* to go talk to some crackpot? You don't need my permission."

"I was hoping you'd come with me," he says so softly that he's almost whispering, and he puts the card back into his wallet where neither of them will have to look at it, stuffs the wallet back into his jeans pocket.

"Well, I won't. I go to your goddamn meetings. I already have to listen to that asshole Zaroba. That's enough for me, thank you very much. That's more than enough."

The little girl petting Dinah slips, loses her footing and almost slides backwards off the edge of the sculpture, but her mother catches her and sets her safely on the ground.

"I see what it's doing to you," Frank says. "I have to watch. How much longer do you think you can go on like this?"

She doesn't answer him, opens her purse and takes out a pack of cigarettes, only one left and she crumbles the empty package and tosses it over her shoulder into the bushes.

"What if this guy really can help you? What if he can make it *stop*?"

Willa is digging noisily around in her purse, trying to find her lighter or a book of matches, and she turns and stares at Frank, the cigarette hanging unlit from her lips. Her eyes shining bright as broken gemstones, shattered crystal eyes, furious, resentful, and he knows then that she could hate him, that she could leave him here and never look back. She takes the cigarette from her mouth, licks her upper lip, and for a long moment Willa holds the tip of her tongue trapped tight between her teeth.

"What the hell makes you think I want it to stop?"

And silence as what she's said sinks in and he begins to understand that he's never understood her at all. "It's killing you," he says, finally, the only thing he can think to say, and Willa's eyes seem to flash and grow brighter, more broken, more eager to slice. "No, Frank, it's the only thing keeping me *alive*. Knowing that it's out there, that I'll see it again, and someday maybe it won't make me come back *here*."

And then she gets up and walks quickly away towards the pond, brisk, determined steps to put more distance between them. She stops long enough to bum a light from an old black man with a dachshund, then ducks around one corner of the boathouse and he can't see her anymore. Frank doesn't follow, sits watching the tiny sailboats and yachts gliding gracefully across the mossdark surface of the water, their silent choreography of wakes and ripples. He decides maybe it's better not to worry about Willa for now, plenty enough time for that later, and he wonders what he'll say to Monalisa when he finds him.

We shall be less apt to admire what this World calls great, shall nobly despise those Trifles the generality of Men set their Affections on, when we know that there are a multitude of such Earths inhabited and adorn'd as well as our own.

Christiaan Huygens (c. 1690)

RICHARD KIRK

THE REST
OF THE WRONG THING

Caitlín R. Kiernan and Poppy Z. Brite

Not quite five miles south of town, and there's nothing much to see this far out, nothing much at all; the forests patiently reclaiming patchwork fields that have lain fallow since Nixon was president, rusted barbed-wire boundaries, the iron rail and creosote-stained crosstie stitches of the Norfolk Southern line. There are still trains, of course, rushing loud across the autumncool Harnett County night, steel centipedes racing obsolescence on their perfect razor feet. And where the tracks pass by the charcoal ruins of the Central Carolina Cotton Mill, Terry Buckett parks his car in the vast gravelpaved lot that once served the mill and the men and women who spent their days and nights there, before the fire of '75.

He turns the key and for a few long moments Terry and Vic and the skinny girl in the back sit together and alone in the darkness left after the head-lights go out, the dark and the comparative silence left after the rumble and growl of the old Rambler's unmuffled V-8 engine. There's a Doors tape in the cassette deck and Jim Morrison's still crooning about The End, his loungesultry voice almost as smooth, as seamless and foreboding as the sky spread out above them, the bright and careless spray of stars and a three-quarter moon, hung high and white and cold.

"Well," Terry says, staring out through the wind-shield at the mill. "This is it."

"Yeah," the skinny girl says. "I know," and Vic mumbles something half to herself, opens the glove compartment and starts digging around inside for the flashlight.

"Kinsey's mother *died* here," Terry says, and now he's watching the girl in the rearview mirror and wishing he had a beer, a bag of weed, anything to take the edge off, wishing Vic hadn't insisted they do this sober. He tries not to notice the yellow shoe box sitting on the seat beside the girl. "And she wasn't the only one, either," he says. "It's not my favorite place to hang out."

The girl glances at him from the backseat, eyes slick and hard as ball bearings, eyes that give noth-ing away and ask for nothing in return. *She's smiling at me*, he thinks. *Laughing at me*, even though he can see perfectly well that she isn't, that her lips, the fine lines around her eyes, are still stuck in the same sour, dissatisfied expression she was wearing when Vic showed up with her at the Sacred Yew.

"Well, if it makes you feel any better, Mr. Buckett, this isn't exactly my idea of a good time," she says dryly, matter-of-factly, and then she looks back toward the ruined and waiting hulk of the mill.

"Jesus, Vic. Will you please tell her to quit calling me that? I already asked her not—"

"Why don't we just get this over with," Vic says and opens her door, climbs out and a gust of the late October night rushes in to fill the empty space she leaves, air that smells like peach cider and Halloween candy, like frost and hay, clean, dry smells to overpower the pot and stale beer funk of the Rambler's upholstery. Vic slams the door behind her and the whole car shudders.

"I think I can finish this on my own," the skinny girl says. "Maybe both of you should wait for me here. It won't take long."

Terry switches off the stereo and turns around in his seat, but the girl doesn't seem to notice, ignores him if she has noticed, doesn't take her pale, steelsecret eyes off the window. She's touching the glass with the tip of one index finger, tracing invisible clockwise swirls, mazes or mandalas against the darkness.

"Hey, I'm no goddamn hero. If I could get Vic back in this car, that's just *exactly* what you'd be doing."

"All I asked for was directions," the girl says. She reaches the center of one of her swirly patterns and her finger reverses direction, going round and round the other way. "I didn't ask you guys to bring me out here."

"Yeah, well, that wasn't my idea either, okay? You can thank Vic for that, too," and now he does look at the box, scuffed and dented shoe box the sticky, unreal color of a banana Popsicle. There are big oily

93

stains on the sides of the box, stains like fried chicken leaking through a paper lunch bag.

"Victoria doesn't really understand any of it," the girl says very quietly. "She wouldn't be trying to help me if she understood. I tried to tell her that. I *showed* her."

"Maybe she understands a whole lot more than you give her credit for," and Terry's glad that he's getting angry, getting righteously pissed off at this creepy girl and her creepy eyes, that fucking yellow shoe box, because it's better to be angry than scared. Out here in the night, better to keep himself busy wishing he'd never seen her, wishing she'd wandered into someone else's life, than to think about what might be waiting for them in the mill, what's hiding beneath the lid of the shoe box.

"Maybe," the girl says. "But I don't think so. I remind her of someone else, that's all."

Yeah. Wednesday fuckin' Addams, he thinks and Terry sighs loudly through his teeth and turns away from the girl. Vic is standing a few feet in front of the car now, trying to get the flashlight to work. She shakes it hard and the bulb winks reluctantly to life, throws an unsteady mask of light and shadow across her face so that he hardly even recognizes her, before it winks out again. And pissed off or not, Terry's starting to feel like the Cowardly Lion at the edge of the Wicked Witch's haunted forest. *I do believe in spooks, I do believe in spooks, I do, I do, I do...*

"We shouldn't let her stand out there by herself. Out in the open like that," the girl says and "Right," Terry Buckett whispers and they both get out of the Rambler.

94

Early Saturday afternoon and Terry was at The Sacred Yew with Kinsey Hummingbird and R.J. and Calvin, everyone wielding paintbrushes, using up the three big cans of cheap, black all-weather latex house paint. The front and back doors were both propped wide open with garbage cans and bricks but the fumes were still making them all goofy. The paint fumes and the beer, cold bottles of Dixie and National Bohemian that Kinsey was giving out free because they'd all volunteered to help without having to be asked.

"No-account, white-trash, racist sonsabitches," R.J. said again, at least the six- or seven-hundredth time he'd said that, or something just like that, since they'd started, and then he dipped his brush in the nearest can. It came out shiny and dripping midnight and he wiped the extra paint off on the edge before turning back to the wall behind the stage. The wall that'd read HIPPIE FREAK SWINE in chalkwhite letters five feet high when they'd started, working from the middle towards either end, and they'd already blacked out enough that it only read HIP and WINE instead.

"Hell, maybe we should leave it like that," Kinsey said, frowning at the violated wall and running one hand's worth of paintscabbed fingers through his long, thinning hair. "It'd be like...well, you know...like finding the truth hidden in the oppression."

"Jesus, Kinsey. I think you need some fresh air," Terry said, setting down his brush. And "Yeah," Kinsey mumbled. "I think you're right."

Terry had been the first to notice that someone had broken into the Yew, the first to see the graffiti; on his way down Firehouse Street to open the Whirling Disc, still half asleep and grumbling about the sun in his eyes, the back of the Rambler loaded down with cardboard boxes of CDs and vinyl and old *Rolling Stone* magazines that he'd picked up the day before at a flea market over in Corinth. And then he'd seen the two huge crimson swastikas spraypainted across the front of the club and almost run off the road into a telephone pole.

"Man, this shit is fuckin' unbelievable," Calvin muttered, lit a cigarette and then he sat down on an old produce crate at the edge of the stage. "I just don't get it, Kinsey. I mean, the assholes didn't even *steal* anything."

Kinsey looked at Calvin and then stared down at the brush in his own hand, the stiff nylon bristles clotted with black paint.

"To tell you the honest truth, I'm surprised it didn't happen a long time ago," he said, and there was a flat, disheartened quality to his voice, a tone Terry couldn't recall ever having heard from Kinsey before.

"You're not going cynical on us, are you?" he asked, and Kinsey shrugged his broad, bony shoulders and dabbed half-heartedly at the wall with his brush.

"Maybe," he said. "Or maybe I'm just getting old. But, hell, sometimes it feels like the world gets a little bit meaner every day I live. Sometimes I feel like I've spent most of my life trying to hide from shit like *this*," and he pokes the wall with his paintbrush for emphasis. "I tried to build a sanctuary, you know, someplace safe—"

"Ain't no place safe," the girl said, and when Terry turned away from Kinsey, there she was, standing beside Vic on the other side of the stage. Small and skinny girl, gaunt girl long past skinny, all angles and jutting bones wrapped up in a faded black Cure T-shirt, her tiny breasts barely even a suggestion of curve beneath Robert Smith's pouting, mascara-smeared face.

"What the hell happened?" Vic asked and pointed at the wall, at HIP and WINE and the fresh paint glistening under the house lights. "There are two big swastikas—"

"Racist sonsabitches," R.J. said, interrupting, as though that were all the explanation needed. He sat down near Calvin.

"Well, has anyone called the cops?" Vic asked and Kinsey nodded.

"Yeah," he said, still dabbing at the wall. "They came and took pictures. Asked some questions. Wanted to know if I had any illegal drugs stashed around the Yew. Or guns. Asked if I was Jewish."

"You're kidding me," she said, sounding annoyed and incredulous at the same time, and glanced over her left shoulder toward the open front door and the two bright red swastikas still waiting outside.

"Afraid not, baby," Terry said. "Who's your friend?"

And Vic turned back and stared at the girl as if she'd forgotten that anyone was standing there next to her, as if, for one moment, she had absolutely no idea *who* the girl was.

"Oh, yeah," she said uncertainly. "Yeah. I'm sorry. This is Tyler. We met over at the diner. She's from Richmond."

"Just *north* of Richmond," the girl corrected her.

"Right. Tyler, this is my boyfriend, Terry Buckett, and that's Calvin and R.J. and Kinsey," pointing at each of them in turn. "Kinsey owns this place."

"It's good to meet you," Tyler said, "All of you," and she bowed her head slightly in their direction. A peculiar gesture from a more peculiar girl, her eyes the color of slate and granite pebbles under icy, flowing water, her long and tangled hair the artificial purple of grape Kool-Aid. "I'm sorry it isn't under more pleasant circumstances," she added, and Terry noticed the yellow shoe box, then, tucked snug under one of Tyler's thin arms. When he looked at Vic again she was watching the floor at her feet, peering into the shadows at the splintery edge of the stage. And the expression on her face, the unaccustomed wariness etched into her skin like a scar, made him want to stop the world, rewind a few hours, and see if there was any way at all to miss whatever weird shit the girl named Tyler signified, whatever was going to happen next.

CRSO

Jesus, Terry thinks. *It looks like some sort of dead monster*; he's got the flashlight now, standing beside Vic and she's holding Tyler's hand again. Nothing left between them and the mill but a broken down chain-link fence, warped and twisted steel wire with plenty of places they can go under or over or straight through. And Terry wishes there weren't. Wishes the fucking fence was fifty feet high, a hundred feet high and topped with coils of razor wire, maybe a few hungry Dobermans on the other side just for good measure. Then he could shrug his shoulders and kick at the gravel, maybe cuss a little bit, a good show of mock disappointment so no one can ever say he's a coward and *Sorry, kiddo. We tried, honest. Did our best. Guess this is as far as we go, hmmm?*

"Oh, I see you in there," the girl says very quietly, almost whispering, staring so intent at the ruins and the mill seems to stare right back at her, at all three of them. The spiteful gaze of empty socket windows and doorways, resentful holes punched in the crumbling, sootblackened brick walls. The sagging sheetmetal roof like the shattered backbone of this terrible place, and the unsteady beam of Terry's flashlight wanders across masonry that winks at him and glistens with a thick, translucent layer of melted glass forever frozen in uneven keloid folds.

"I *know* exactly what you did," Tyler says. "So don't go pretending for a second that I don't," and her voice is rising like she's afraid of being misunderstood or afraid the mill can't hear at all. Terry glances at Vic, because she *has* to see how fucked-up this has gotten, never mind what's in that yellow shoe box or any of the crazy bullshit the girl's told them since the Yew. But Vic is busy watching Tyler scolding phantoms and she doesn't even see him.

"Used to be farms here," the girl says to the mill and she points to the limestone gravel at her feet. "Used to be people to work the land. But you never wanted people, did you? Just stinking, clanking machines and enough hands to keep them running night and day —"

"Excuse me a second," Terry says, as the flashlight bulb flickers and dies again. "Is this sermon absolutely fucking necessary?" He shakes the flashlight, smacks one end of it hard against his palm, but it doesn't come back on.

"*Listen,*" the girl hisses and cocks her head to one side like a curious dog and "Can't you *hear* it?" she asks.

And Terry Buckett *does* hear it then, and he stops wrestling with the traitorous flashlight and stands very still, the pins-and-needles prickle of goose bumps washing hot and cold across his arms, the fine hairs on the back of his neck standing suddenly at attention; feeling like a jackass for being afraid and knowing damn well it doesn't matter how he feels, because he does hear the noises coming from the burned-out mill.

"What the hell is it?" Vic asks and Tyler lets go of her hand, reaches out and her fingertips brush the chain-link fence. She closes her eyes and holds the shoe box close to her chest.

"Just old memories," Tyler tells her. "Bad memories. All it ever wanted and all it's ever gonna have."

The clanking wheeze and geartooth clamor of the looms, tireless machinery tongues and the fainter, weary voices of the pickers, the weavers, a slamming door, breaking glass, and Terry takes a step back, away from the mill. But the sounds are still there, must have been there all along but he never would have noticed them on his own. One dry, onionskin layer of the night peeled back and this is what was buried underneath. Not even a ghost, but something worse, something vast and mindless and you can't even say it's lost because no one's ever looked for it.

"C'mon, Vic," he says. "We're going back to the car."

Tyler opens her pebblecolored eyes and looks at him doubtfully. Vic's still staring at the mill, her lips slack and she hasn't moved an inch.

"Can't you hear me? I said we're going back to the car."

"I heard you," Vic says and Terry glances over his shoulder at the Rambler waiting alone in the middle of the parking lot. The car looks small and very, very far away.

"Then what the fuck are you waiting for?"

"I can't let her do this by herself," Vic says. "That's what it wants, isn't it? It's a bully and it wants us to run off and leave Tyler alone," and then she ducks through a narrow, jagged tear in the chain link before he can stop her, before he can even say anything else. She pauses a moment on the other side and looks back at him.

"I'm sorry, Terry," Vic says and then she's gone, turns and slips quickly away into the shadows, through a doorway and leaves him standing there with the girl named Tyler and her stupid yellow shoe box.

"I didn't make her do that," Tyler says and he shakes his head, trying not to hear the clatter of dead machines, the murmur of dead men and women.

"Yeah," he says. "I know. Vic's plenty capable of doing stupid shit on her own," and then he helps Tyler through the tear in the fence and they follow Victoria into the darkness.

⊰⊱

After they left the Yew, left Kinsey and R.J. and Calvin still painting the walls black again because maybe HIP and WINE didn't look so good after all, and there were still the big red swastikas to deal with. The three of them in Terry's two-toned Rambler, three-toned if you counted all the rusty patches, turquoise above, white below a strip of dingy chrome, and Terry behind the wheel. Vic was sitting next to him and the girl named Tyler riding along in the back seat, all those boxes crammed in behind her, the flea-market goodies he still hadn't unloaded.

"Calvin thinks it was just kids," Terry said. "Probably just a couple of drunk jocks from Corinth or Duncan, but R.J.'s pretty sure it was a whole pack of skins from Raleigh. He said he read something in the newspaper last week about a big skinhead jamboree up in Raleigh."

"I don't think they call them jamborees," Vic said and she opened a new pack of Camels, crumpled the cellophane wrapping and dropped it to the floorboard along with all the other garbage there. "That's the Boy Scouts."

"Same damn difference," Terry said, smiled at Victoria, and he turned off Firehouse Street, bumped into the narrow cobblestone alley behind the Whirling Disc.

Tyler sighed loudly from the back seat, sudden, windy sound like maybe someone had jabbed her too hard with something sharp and her soul was rushing out through the puncture.

"Why do you assume *they* came from somewhere else?" she said. "Why couldn't it have been someone from this town? Or don't you have hate here?"

102

Terry shook his head and pulled over behind the record shop, maneuvering the rear end of the Rambler as close to the back door of the Disc as he dared. He wrestled the stick into park and killed the motor.

"I think if anyone in Missing Mile was going to trash the Yew, they'd have done it a long time ago," he said, talking to the girl through the rear-view mirror. "Nope. These fuckers were most definitely outsiders."

"You're sure of that, Mr. Buckett?"

"Pretty sure, yeah. And don't call me Mr. Buckett."

"Well, that's what everyone always wants to believe, isn't it?" Tyler asked his reflection, but it wasn't really a question, the smug certainty on her face to say she already knew the answer, the only answer she wanted, anyway. "The bad shit always comes from somewhere else. From *outside* us. Outside our world. At least, that's what we'd like to think. That's why *Dracula* has always been so much more popular than Jekyll and Hyde. But werewolves are a lot scarier than vampires, even if no one wants to admit it."

"Werewolves...Christ, Vic. Where the hell did you find this kid?" Terry asked. "Too bad Ghost isn't around. He'd love her."

She shrugged once, smiled at him nervously, and took a long drag off her cigarette. "More like she found me," Vic said, a puff of guarded, smoky words, and then she got out of the car.

The girl helped them unload the Rambler, helped haul the heavy boxes of LPs and tattered old magazines into the back room of the shop, stuffy, dusthaunted space that doubled as a stockroom and a warehouse for half the bands in town. Confusion

103

of shipping crates and busted amps, unopened boxes of Whirling Disc t-shirts, microphone stands and unstackable stacks of posters piled high like a hoard of impossibly glossy, ancient scrolls.

Terry set the last of the *Rolling Stone*s down beside the discarded shell of a Fender Rhodes 88 electric piano that had been stripped for parts years and years ago. The Smashing Pumpkins, tricked out in their best glam rags, stared up at him from the cover of the topmost magazine.

"Show him," Vic said to the girl and he turned around, his back aching a little, just enough to remind him that the years and his wicked ways, his layabout pothead lifestyle, were starting to catch up with him. "Show me what?" he asked them and Tyler looked reluctantly down at the yellow shoe box in her hands.

"Are you *sure*?" and Victoria nodded her head.

"He won't ever believe you, otherwise," she said.

Tyler glanced from the box to Vic and then back to the box again.

"All I wanted was directions to the mill — "

"But I'm not going to let you go out there by yourself," Vic said and lit another cigarette. "I already told you that. So you might as well show him."

"Will one of you please tell me what the fuck you're talking about? Show me *what*, for Christ's sake?"

The girl took a very deep breath, drawing breath like someone about to dive into water that's deep and black and freezing cold, and she opened the yellow shoe box.

"There used to be a cotton mill near here," she said. "The Central Carolina Cotton Mill," but Terry wasn't really paying attention, looking at the object in the box instead. Something not much larger than a spark plug, wrapped in an oily swatch of blue gingham cloth.

"My grandfather worked there," Tyler said. "He was working there when it burned down twenty-five years ago."

And then she took the ginghamswaddled object from the shoe box, passed the box to Vic, and peeled back the greasy-looking fabric.

"He was one of the lucky ones," she said, the bitter inflection tacked on "lucky" so Terry knew that wasn't really the word she meant at all. "He didn't die in the fire. He died from lung cancer a few years ago, but he had brown lung for half his life. Byssinosis —"

"I *know* what brown lung is," Terry muttered, and he was beginning to think this was some kind of dumb practical joke, Vic's half-assed idea of a prank, the way the girl was taking her own sweet time unwrapping the thing from the box, handling it like dynamite or a baby rattlesnake.

"He worked the card room," she said and gingerly pulled the last thin layer of gingham back so that he could see the thing cradled in her palm. "He always said that carding was one of the most dangerous jobs in the mill, what with all those belts and pulleys and drive shafts going a mile a minute —"

"So what's it supposed to be?" Terry asked her, and at first it really didn't look like much of anything at all; two, maybe three inches of twisted, amber-colored glass or plastic, translucent or nearly so, and the end pointing toward her fingertips, toward him, threaded like a screw and what looked like a short

105

length of rusty wire wound tightly, haphazardly, around the threads.

"He went back, a couple months after the fire, to put some flowers where some of his friends died," Tyler said, and held the thing out so that Terry could get a closer look at it in the dim light of the stockroom. "That's when he found it. Or it found him."

The other end of the thing wasn't threaded, or if it had been once upon a time, it wasn't anymore. The amber-colored stuff tapered down to a point, and that part of it looked almost organic, like the writhing head of a worm frozen in place, or a discarded appendage from one of the impossible alien creatures in John Carpenter's remake of *The Thing*. *No*, he thought, *that's not it at all*, remembering pictures from a book by Stephen Jay Gould, a book about the things that had lived at the bottom of the ocean five hundred million years before the dinosaurs. Things with all-too appropriate names like *Hallucigenia* and *Anomalocaris*, animals that might have been built by H. R. Giger instead of natural selection.

"It's *wrong*," she said. "You can see that, can't you?"

And Terry shook his head no, shook his head again and "It's just a melted piece of glass or ceramic," he said. "Sure, it's weird-looking, but it's still just a piece of junk. It might have been part of a fuse or electric insulator and then the fire must have melted it and—"

"No," Tyler said.

And something began to drip through her fingers, a dark and viscous substance like dirty motor oil that fell slower than it should have, as though the air around the droplets was too thick or gravity too weak.

Small, oildark stains at her feet and when Terry looked back up at the thing it seemed to shimmer, the same way hot asphalt shimmers on a summer day, and the end pointing toward the girl, the end like the head of some Pre-Cambrian sea slug, had begun to writhe.

"That's enough," Victoria said and shoved the box at Tyler. "Put it back. Make it stop."

"Are you sure?" the girl whispered, taunting whisper and she didn't take the box or even glance at Vic, keeping her eyes fixed on Terry. He could feel the fat beads of sweat popping out on his upper lip, the sweat starting to trickle down his forehead to sting his eyes. His stomach felt the way it did when he had a particularly bad headache or a hangover, and "Yeah," he said, "Put it back, Tyler," croaking because his mouth had suddenly gone dry, and he swallowed once, twice, forcing a stingy bit of spit down his parched throat.

"But you *do* see it now?" she said to him. "You do *see* that it's wrong," and he nodded his head quickly and looked away from the thing in her hand, looked at Vic, but she was staring up at the ceiling of the stockroom.

"Hurry, Tyler. Please," and there was a sound somewhere high above them, a sound like thunder or someone tearing a head of cabbage in half, both those sounds at the same time and not exactly either one. The air smelled hot, ozone hot stink and the fainter stench of rotting meat.

"Sometimes things pass too close to us," Tyler said. "Things from other places. Machineries of blood and starlight. *Wrong* things."

"Oh, Jesus, Tyler. Put it back in the box," and there were tears on Vic's face, streaking her pale cheeks.

"Just put it back in the motherfucking box before it's too late."

Terry looked up at the ceiling, searching the place that Vic was watching like she'd just seen the Miracle of Fatima, like there was a goddamned UFO hovering directly above their heads, and all he could see was the dusty fluorescent light fixture, the high ceiling and in spots the plaster had long ago cracked and fallen away, exposing the lathe underneath. But nothing to explain her tears or the bottomless dread in her green eyes, nothing he could see.

And then Tyler wrapped the writhing thing up in the stained piece of blue gingham again, took the box from Vic's shaking hands, and put the little bundle back inside.

"I'm sorry," she said, and the bitterness and sarcasm were gone, nothing left in her voice but regret. "I didn't want to do that, Mr. Buckett. I swear to God, I never wanted to let it do that again."

The tearing, thundersky sounds had stopped, and the smells were gone, too, if there had ever been any smells, if he'd really heard anything at all. Terry sat down on a gutted Marshall amp and wiped the sweat from his face, blinked, but the oily splotches at Tyler's feet were still there.

"I have to take it back where it came from," she said. "It does...things when I'm not watching and I *can't* watch it all the time. I can't watch it forever."

Terry looked at Vic, her face hidden in her hands now, ashamed or sobbing and he couldn't quite tell which. Both maybe, and "Are you okay?" he asked her. For an answer she turned away, took a step toward the door to the alley.

"I'm sorry," Tyler said again and then none of them said anything else for a while.

CRSD

Whatever the inside of the mill had been like before the fire, now it was something else entirely, grotesque landscape shaped by heat and moonlight and twenty-five years of exposure to the harsh Carolina summers and winters, frost and sun, rain and the gnawing jaws of insects. Terry continued to fumble with the flashlight as he followed the girl through the maze of wrecked machinery and scorched timber, switching it on and off, on and off, to no avail. Maybe the batteries were dead, or the bulb had blown out. Maybe it wasn't enough that he was probably about to die in this shithole, trip over something and break his fucking neck, wind up with a rusty nail through his forehead, maybe the gods had decided he had to do it in the dark.

"Wait *up*, dammit," he shouts at Tyler, and Terry can just make out her silhouette somewhere up ahead, ten or twenty feet to the blacker shape of her body outlined against a heap of ruined looms and spoolers.

"Hurry," she says, whispering like she's afraid someone's listening.

"Where the hell is Vic?" he snaps at her and something sharp snags at the legs of his jeans, catches the left cuff and he has to pull hard to get free. There's the ragged sound of cloth ripping, too loud in the night, in the stillness of the wasted mill. He thinks maybe his leg is scraped, too, and tries not to think about staph infections and tetanus shots.

109

"Vic!" he yells. "Victoria! Where *are* you?!" and what's left of the ceiling and brick walls bounce the question right back at him, not exactly an echo, some weirder, sonic ricochet. When Tyler tugs at the sleeve of his jacket he almost screams.

"I don't think she can hear you, Mr. Buckett," the girl whispers, urgent and frightened whisper, and "But please stop yelling. It might be listening," she says.

"*What* might be listening, Tyler? What are you talking about?" and now there's a burning pain in his left leg somewhere just above the ankle, warm trickle of blood into his left tennis shoe, so at least he can stop wondering whether or not he's cut. "Jesus, this is stupid. No. This is *worse* than stupid. This is fucking crazy," and Tyler tugs at his sleeve again.

"Just follow me," she says. "We'll find her. I promise."

"Thanks a bunch," Terry grumbles, staring glumly down at his wounded ankle lost somewhere in the inky darkness pooled on the concrete floor. "You *promise*. That makes me feel a whole hell of a lot better."

But he does follow her, holds her hand as the girl named Tyler picks her way through the tangled maze of metal and splintered wood like she's done this a thousand times, knows the way better than the back of her hand and could do this in her sleep. Across a wide, junkcluttered cement plain, the air stinking of burned wood and grease and chemicals, bales of cotton still rotting after two and a half decades.

There are probably rats, too, Terry thinks. *Great big, fat, rabies-carrying, plague-infected rats.*

"Here," Tyler says, "She went down that way, down to the basement," and he can see that they've stopped at a wall, charred cinder blocks and mortar and no window.

But there wouldn't be a window, would there? Surely we haven't gone nearly far enough to be all the way at the back of the building.

"Well, I don't see jack shit," he says and so she points at the floor a few feet to their right.

"Right *there*, Mr. Buckett," and his heart skips a beat or two when he finally sees the hole; not so dark here, enough moonlight leaking through what's left of the roof for him to tell where the floor ends, and he can even make out the first few stairs leading down into the most perfect darkness he's ever dared imagine.

"Jesus," and now he's whispering, too. "Are you telling me Vic went down *there*?"

"That's where it all started, I think, in the basement," Tyler says. "The epicenter must be down there somewhere. Victoria's too sensitive to be this close to it. I shouldn't have ever let her come."

"No, I don't think she would have gone down there. Vic's too afraid of spiders and—"

"Be quiet," the girl says and crouches down next to the entrance to the basement. "Do you hear that?"

And at first he doesn't hear anything but the gentle October breeze slipping around all the slicing edges of the mill, crickets, a night bird calling somewhere far across the fields. All the things he *should* be hearing, but then Tyler leans closer to the hole in the floor, cups a hand around her right ear, and *there* it is, a faint, splashing noise and something else, something he's never heard before and probably couldn't begin to describe if his life depended on it.

At the entrance to the basement, Tyler makes a dry sound that's either a laugh or a sigh, and "Down, down, *down*," she says, not bothering to whisper anymore. "I wonder how many miles I've fallen by this time? I must be getting somewhere near the center of the earth—"

"You're off your fucking nut, kiddo," he says and she turns her head and gazes back at him over her shoulder. And for a second her eyes seem to flash a brilliant, iridescent green, cat eyes caught in the headlights of an oncoming car. But only a second, half a second, and then they're as secret, as dim, as any human eyes lost in this dark place.

"You don't know," she says. " You don't know anything. If you *did*..." but Tyler doesn't finish, stands up again, the yellow shoe box clutched close to her chest, and she goes down without him.

At the bottom of the stairs, the flooded basement, and Terry stands in the chilly water that comes almost all the way up to his knees. He can see just fine now and wishes that he couldn't, knows he'll never be able to *stop* seeing this, that whenever he closes his eyes this will always be there, waiting for him.

Beneath a labyrinth of rusting pipes, dangling iron and PVC maze suspended from the concrete ceiling, Tyler stands by herself in the water, almost as high as her waist. The shoe box and its lid float nearby like tiny yellow boats and she's holding the thing in both her hands, the way old women hold dowsing rods. That's where the light is coming from, from the wormheaded end of the thing, the *wrong* thing, and that end pointed straight ahead of her, toward nothing but the last cringing shadows at the back of the basement.

"Terry? Is that you? Is that *really* you?" Vic says and Terry looks frantically about for a moment before he finds her, huddled only a few feet away from him between an old filing cabinet and the moldscabbed wall. "I thought you were going to *leave* me here," she says, her voice trembling and unbelieving, desolate and relieved.

He splashes clumsily towards her, trips and drops the useless flashlight, almost falls facedown in the filthy water. But she catches him, and her hands are like flesh carved from living ice. Her teeth chattering and she holds onto him, sobbing loudly now, and buries her face in the folds of his shirt and jacket.

"Jesus, Vic. You know I wouldn't have left you here," he says, his lips pressed against her ear, and she shakes her head. "No," she says, "I *didn't* know. I didn't know anything anymore."

And he looks at the girl again, the light around her grown so bright that he has to squint, shades his eyes with one hand. The amber thing wriggles and twists in her hands, seems to be *stretching*, and it's almost impossible to tell where the thing ends and the light begins. The sound from before, the impossible sound, is everywhere, so loud, so absolute, it could drown them as surely as the water lapping at his pants legs. The light flows away from Tyler in dazzling tendrils, the unfathomably intricate roots or nervous system of a creature *made* of light, photon dendrites filling up the basement and the air crackles and spits electric fire.

The girl turns her head towards Terry and Vic, and he can see her lips moving, her mouth forming

113

words, but it's hard to hear her over the noise. Her eyes flash green again and the light swells, doubles, trebles, so bright that he has to close his eyes, has to look away.

Run, she says and he doesn't pause to wonder that her voice is *inside* his head, hearing her clearly now but not with his ears. Hearing her with his soul or some gray scrap of his brain he's never used before.

I have to take it back where it came from, all the way back. Run, Mr. Buckett. Get Victoria out of here.

He glances at the stairs and then back to the girl, squints painfully at the light coiling taut about her like a cocoon and the thing from the shoe box whips madly back and forth in her hands, an amber blur vomiting fire and thunder.

Hurry. I can't wait much longer. It's opening.

So he goes, one arm linked so tight around Vic's waist that she'll have bruises for weeks. He pulls her from the flooded basement, stumbling up the cement stairs to the scorched ruins of the mill and then back across the gravel parking lot to the Rambler. Terry only looks back once, remembering childhood Bible stories about Lot's wife and pillars of salt; only looks back when he hears Tyler start to scream, but there's nothing to see, nothing but the silent, brooding hulk of the Central Carolina Cotton Mill and the indifferent carpet of stars spread out overhead.

ᏆᏇ

And in the hazythick weeks that follow, long days passing like refrigerated honey or maple syrup, Terry spends more and more time alone in the Whirling Disc.

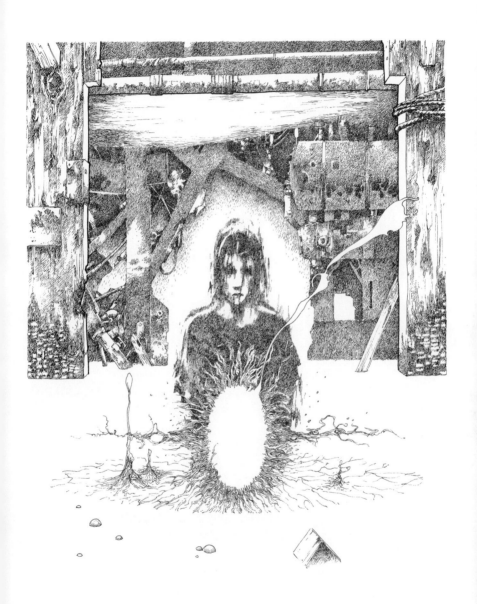

RICHARD KIRK

The doors rarely unlocked and the faded sign always turned to the side that reads BACK IN 5…OR 15…OR WHENEVER. Sometimes he thinks about scrawling JUST FUCK OFF on the sign with a Magic Marker and maybe then he can stop hiding in the stockroom whenever kids show up and bang on the glass, wanting in, wanting the new Limp Bizkit or Eminem or Kid Rock CD, the stupid shit teenagers listen to these days. He doesn't like the stockroom anymore. There are ugly stains on the floor, stains like oil, but no matter how many times he scrubs them, no matter if he uses soap or Pine-Sol or gasoline, the stains stay right there, indelible, tattooed deep into the cement.

Vic didn't leave until he told her to, finally, when he couldn't stand her crying any longer, or the blank and empty look in her eyes, the way she'd sit behind the counter for hours, perfectly quiet, perfectly still, staring out the front of the shop at Firehouse Street.

"She isn't ever coming back," Terry said one day and when Vic started crying he asked her to leave. She didn't argue. Hardly a word between them since the night at the mill anyway, and she wouldn't even let him touch her. Not that he'd been in the mood for sex, but the way she lay awake in bed night after night, her back turned to him while she mumbled to herself about angels and lightning, had started to get on his nerves. She left Missing Mile, went to stay with her mother in Charleston, he thinks.

He drinks too much, George Dickel and Jack Daniels and hardly ever any weed. Plays the same Billie Holiday record over and over because he can't stand the silence, what seems to be waiting for him somewhere just behind the silence. The memory of a sound, and whenever Kinsey comes around to see if

117

he's still breathing, to bring him food and Thermoses of hot, black coffee, Terry tries to think of normal things to talk about. The weather or music, shit like that, tries hard to pay attention to the things that Kinsey tells him. That he should lay off the booze, that maybe he should think about getting help, that he should call Vic.

And something the girl said keeps coming back, lines from *Alice in Wonderland,* and he's written it down in the back of a thick, spiral-bound notebook that Victoria left behind.

I wonder how many miles I've fallen by this time? I must be getting somewhere near the center of the earth.

Red ink on college-ruled pages, and he has a cheap Dover paperback of Lewis Carroll. Has highlighted a lot of things that Tyler *didn't* say, but that seem to matter anyway.

— that's about the right distance — but then I wonder what Latitude or Longitude I've got to?

He also has an old *Time* atlas which he keeps on the counter beside the register, keeps open to page five and a circular map of the world as seen from the North Pole, the pole as precise mathematical center; a small red dot to mark the approximate position of Missing Mile and an eight-inch red line drawn to a point on the other side of the earth, his best guess for what's on the other side, directly opposite if you could dig your way through the crust and the mantle and the outer core. Digging all the way to China, the Min River north of Chengtu, to be exact.

And one late December day on his way in from Violin Road to the Disc he parks the Rambler outside the small, whitewashed brick building on one corner side of the town square, combination city hall and post of-

118

fice and public library. Stops because the library has a computer, a fancy, new Macintosh and anyone is allowed to use it. It only takes him forty-five minutes to find what he's looking for, searching dozens of ufology and conspiracy theory websites, websites devoted to the paranormal, the unexplained, and there it is: July 5th, 1975 — July 6th, in China — an explosion in the sky above Chengtu that was heard as far away as Shanghai, that rattled seismometer needles in Chungking and Sian. A cloud over the city the color of opium poppies and then a black, oily rain that lasted for almost an hour.

Down, down, down...

Sometimes things pass too close to us. Machineries of blood and starlight.

He sits on the stool in front of the computer until an old black man in overalls and a green and yellow John Deere cap, loose-fitting dentures, asks if Terry is done, and yes, he says and apologizes for making the man wait so long.

Outside, the air smells a little like Christmas, crisp and sweet. There's a quarter in the pocket of his jeans and he crosses the street to a pay phone, dials information and when the operator comes on the line and asks what city, he says Charleston.

He isn't surprised when Vic answers the phone at her mother's house.

"Black bodies and the dark rabbles of the sky — and that rioting thing, from floating anarchies..."

Charles Fort, *New Lands* (1923)

Afterword:
Reflections on a Wrong Thing

Caitlín R. Kiernan

Perhaps you are not the sort of person who en-
joys reading about how a short story came to be written. I've certainly known lots of people who aren't,
people who generally find all such anecdotes tiresome
or conceited or somehow deleterious to the effect of
the story itself, and so tend to avoid introductions,
prologues, forewords, afterwords, endnotes, appen-
dices, etc., like the proverbial plague, whether the
material in question was written by the author or by
someone else.[1] In college, I once heard a student de-

---

[1] I had a few disparaging words of my own for afterwords in
particular, in the afterword I wrote for *Are You Loathsome Tonight?* In hindsight, though, I think that had more to do with not
being in the mood to write an afterword at the time than any
actual disdain for afterwords.

clare, "I can't stand having someone tell me what I'm about to read, or try to explain to me what I've just read." That's a peculiarly late Twentieth-Century American attitude, I suspect, part and parcel of our sometimes misplaced egalitarianism.

Personally, though, I often find the *process* of art far more interesting than the actual *product* of art, that static, *finished*-thing which we usually think of as "artwork." But it is the process, of course, which is the truer "work of art" and, I believe, often critical to fully understanding a painting or novel or poem or what have you (and Cleanth Brooks, John Crowe Ransom, and the rest of the New Critics be damned). Perhaps this is one reason that I'm such a great admirer of the writing of Kathe Koja, an author who, in novels like *Strange Angels* and *Skin*, has often explored the artistic process, its consequences to the artist, and the oddly emptied, diminished, or dissatisfied feelings that often accompany "completion."

So, if you only came for the main attraction and would rather not meet the man with his hand up Yoda's butt, so to speak, you may now proceed without guilt to The Great Egress (or to the back of the line, if you'd like to ride again).[2]

What follows is for me and Poppy and all the rest of you.

CR£O

I first learned of The Wrong Thing on or about October 16th, 2000, in a post by Poppy to

_____

[2]And do *not* e-mail me to tell me how much you hated this afterword, or the footnotes, for that matter.

122

alt.books.cait-r-kiernan, in which she described the contents of a curio cabinet in her home in New Orleans. And thanks to the internet search engine, Google.com (via the recently deceased Deja.com), which continues to see fit to archive and display the writings of millions of people without their permission and regardless of copyright laws, I was able to track down that post:

I have prepared a complete inventory. The cabinet itself is coffin-shaped, glass-fronted, decorated with metal milagros and tiny dried rosebuds. I bought it at the Westgate Gallery – not sure if Leilah Wendell made it or if she was selling them for someone else.

- *My friend Jaysin's forehead tumor in formaldehyde (benign)*
- *Human fetus, male, 12 weeks, also in formaldehyde, very old, in vitrine*
- *Porcelain rose from Paris cemetery (I didn't steal it; my editor did when I said I liked them)*
- *Small Kali idol*
- *Black glitter Matchbox limo*
- *Object from another dimension, a.k.a. "The Wrong Thing" – I cannot describe it; you would go mad*
- *Old-fashioned porcelain chef doll from a king cake*
- *Cat skull (not one of mine)*
- *Dollar-kitty by Cleve*
- *Bronze Egyptian cat*
- *Little clay cat painted with black glitter nail polish given to me by a fan in Melbourne, Oz*
- *Devotional cards from our friend Jason's funeral (not the one with the tumor – he's fine)*

- *Visiting card inscribed with the name of my house's previous owner — he planted the 50-year-old camellias in our yard, and right after we moved in, the card appeared in the bedroom on the night the camellias bloomed*
- *Dried rose from a bouquet Chris gave me*
- *Rosary made of dried rose petals from St. Marco's Cathedral, Venice*
- *Bronze Ganesh idol*
- *Crystal Ganesh idol*
- *Doll made by Dame Darcy*

But the item on this list that most seemed to interest the newsgroup was, not surprisingly, "The Wrong Thing." There were several requests for more information, to which Poppy eventually responded with the following description:

OK, stop reading if you want to stay sane: The Wrong Thing is a small object I found at an abandoned, burned-down amusement park near the New Orleans lakefront when J. K. Potter was photographing me there. It is two or three inches long, twisted as if writhing, made of a hard amber-colored substance that looks sort of like glass (but I don't think it is glass). It has a pointy worm-like head and threads like a screw and a bit of rusty wire wrapped around one end. It looks a little like those drawings of microscopic prehistoric life forms you see in books by Stephen Jay Gould, and it causes mystification and dread in all who see it.[3]

---

[3]At which point I think I advised Poppy that The Wrong Thing might be something as prosaic as a blown electrical conductor, a suggestion she sensibly rejected.

Someone, frustrated by this tantalizing description of a thing which could very clearly never be done justice by mere words, soon requested that Poppy photograph the object and make the photograph available online, to which she then wrote:

I'm afraid. I've heard that when you photograph a thing, sometimes other dimensions are revealed. Like those photos where ghosts appear even though the people in the photos didn't see them. I'm not sure I want to see the rest of the Wrong Thing.

It was at this point that some part of my psyche sat up and took notice, or perhaps some dank, inner convolution of my brain twitched, and "A-ha!" I said (well, it probably wasn't "A-ha" per se, and I don't think I actually said it aloud, but it was something of the sort and I'm sure you get the general idea). Regrettably, stories rarely ever occur to me *as* stories, conveniently stocked with the requisite characters, plots, themes, subplots, settings, etc., but more often begin as an isolated image or phrase, a sticky, little nucleus about which events and personalities slowly begin to adhere. Something about which I start to obsess, to worry, to pick at even though I know if I don't leave it alone it'll never heal. An image like Poppy's reluctant description of "The Wrong Thing" or a phrase exactly like "...the rest of the Wrong Thing."

At the time, I was finishing work on my second short story collection, *From Weird and Distant Shores*, and the publisher had requested a new piece which would be original to the collection. Since much of the book consisted of stories I'd written for "shared-world" anthologies (i.e., stories set in the literary universes of other authors), this seemed like an opportunity for Poppy and me to finally collaborate on a story set in her fictional North Carolina town of Missing Mile. It's something that we'd talked about since at least the summer of 1994, shortly after I moved from Birmingham to Athens, but, for one reason or another, we'd never actually gotten around to doing. So, I called Poppy and suggested a story titled (what else) "The Rest of the Wrong Thing," centering on two minor characters from *Lost Souls* and *Drawing Blood*, Terry Buckett and his girlfriend, Vic. She liked the idea, though I suspect all this attention to the dread Wrong Thing was making her much more than a little nervous, and we agreed I would write the first draft.

I began working on the story on October 18th and managed to finish the first draft by November 7th. It was a moderately easy birth, as such things tend to go for me. I was able to turn a simple aside in *Drawing Blood* (the fact that Kinsey Hummingbird's mother had died in a cotton mill fire in July of 1975[4]) into the foundation for a piece that seemed to capture the Flannery O'Connor-meets-William S. Burroughs essence of Poppy's North Carolina and blend it with themes that are probably more my own.

I have a serious and ongoing love affair with urban archaeology and the ruins of the Machine Age; abandoned industrial sites are a recurring motif in

---

[4]*Drawing Blood*, p. 25 (hb edition, Delacorte Press, November 1993).

my writing, in short stories such as "Glass Coffin" and "Between the Gargoyle Trees," in my comics scripts (see *The Dreaming* #18 and #39, for example), and, to a lesser degree, in my novels.

This fascination is at least two-fold. On the one hand, there's the simple, obvious beauty of decay, the hulking symmetry of a dilapidated steel mill or shipyard and all the countless hues that seem to arise solely from rust and the corruption of metals, from the secret alchemy of iron, rainwater, and time. On the other hand, there's the symbolic importance of these ruins, signifying as they do a more general decay that it often seems to me is the most striking legacy of the last one hundred years. Regardless, I've always selected these places as the most appropriate landscapes for my fiction, serving to underscore the despair and waste of many of my characters.

In "The Rest of the Wrong Thing," I saw a chance to work simultaneously with a rural Southern setting (which I've only rarely done, despite the time that I've lived in such surroundings) and industrial ruin. The thought of the burned-out Central Carolina Cotton Mill, sitting alone and unoccupied except perhaps for bums and wild animals, was irresistible. A cliché of that subspecies of the ghost story, the haunted house story, is the climactic destruction of the "sick house" (to borrow Shirley Jackson's metaphor) in a cathartic, cleansing fire. But here, I thought, is a place that has gone through the fire and surely it must *still* be haunted, as anyone with eyes for ghosts should be able to see. Indeed, here is a place haunted *because* of the fire, which instead of cleansing, has stained this patch of ground near Missing Mile. The setting is made all the more *apropos* by the real Wrong

Thing's discovery at "an abandoned, burned-down amusement park."

In the end, I was fairly happy with the story and, much to my relief, so was Poppy. But at roughly 7,500 words and growing (as Poppy began her work on it), "The Rest of the Wrong Thing" was somewhat longer than what I'd envisioned for the closing story for *From Weird and Distant Shores*. It felt more to me like a whole new act than a finale and I suggested to Poppy that we might perhaps make "The Rest of the Wrong Thing" the centerpiece of a chapbook, provided we could find a publisher who was interested in the project. We quickly found just such a publisher in Bill Schafer at Subterranean Press.

However, this left *FWADS* still shy its last story and we'd already promised my publisher (the now-defunct Sideshow Books[5]) a PZB/CRK collaboration. At this point, I proposed that we write *another* Missing Mile story. Once again, Poppy agreed, and on November 9th, just two days after completing the original draft of "The Rest of the Wrong Thing," I began work on "Night Story, 1973," a shorter short story that turned out to be a sort of prequel to *Lost Souls*. Drawing heavily from my own childhood in rural Alabama, and Poppy's in North Carolina, it gave us the chance to explore Ghost's childhood and his relationship with his grandmother, the wise and witchy Miz Deliverance.

Which brings me, more or less, to the end of the story of how the disturbing bit of wire and melted

---

[5]As it turned out, after difficulties with Sideshow Books, *FWADS* would also go to Subterranean Press.

glass (or *not*-glass, as Poppy will tell you) became the first collaboration between Poppy and me. When I originally suggested a chapbook built around "The Rest of the Wrong Thing," I saw it as a project concerned almost exclusively with that one story. However, the distance between the giddy, headlong "Hey, wouldn't *this* be cool —" stage of any given project and its completion, and the degree to which the initial concept is likely to evolve during that time, is usually enormous. So it really came as no surprise to me that the book Poppy and I eventually agreed to do for Subterranean Press used "The Rest of the Wrong Thing" more as a starting point than a centerpiece.

As of this writing, I've still not seen The Wrong Thing for myself. Perhaps it's better that way.

Caitlín R. Kiernan
1 May 2001
Birmingham, Alabama